*"The more I know of the world,
the more I am convinced that I shall never
see a man whom I can really love.
I require so much!"*

Sense and Sensibility by Jane Austen 1811

Too Many Men

by

Kate Fitzroy

KateFizroy2019©

Prologue

I lay on my back and thought about England. Did I miss it and everyone I knew there? I stared into the darkness for several minutes, but I was too tired to answer my own questions. I turned on my side, curled up and sank into a light, dreamless sleep.

When next I awoke, daylight was glinting through the shutters. My first thought was that the window was on the wrong side of the room. My bedroom, the bedroom of my childhood home, had faced west and never enjoyed the sunrise. I rolled onto my back and considered the matter. Of course, I was in Italy and not at home in Newmarket. The June sunshine, brighter than anything English, touched now upon the gold and faded blues and pinks of the ceiling. I stretched luxuriously in the large double bed and watched as the scene of dancing cherubs gradually brightened. Italy... Renaissance land of frescoed ceilings and terracotta floors. Now I was fully awake, but still, I lay on my back. As the plump-winged cherubs danced above me, their blonde curls dusted with gold, I again thought about England and then, inevitably, about Hughie.

I gave a heavy sigh. I was not exactly a runaway bride. I hadn't fled from the church in my wedding dress, but I had been at the second fitting stage. My best friend, Louisa, had been chosen as chief bridesmaid and was highly excited and planning some secret hen party. Plans had been entrenched, a date set firm and my mother had long been involved in an intense flurry of 'keeping things simple'. I closed my eyes and saw her face. A good, almost beautiful face, unlined by worry or cares. When I told her that I couldn't and wouldn't marry Hugh, she had been shocked… horrified. Her eyes had stretched wide, her mouth had fallen open, and for one moment, I thought she would strike me or faint away. I had never seen her like it before, and the enormity of my decision hit me then. Not marry my Hughie? It did seem impossible. We had been engaged for four years… four reasonably happy years. There had been no arguments or any disruption in our Suffolk lives. Hugh had his beloved horses, and I had my Italian studies. It did seem impossible that I would not become his wife and yet… and yet I had suddenly known it was impossible.

'Do you Verity Rose Gresham take Hugh Charles Farley-Brown as your lawful husband, to have and to hold, from this day forward, for better or for worse, for richer or for poorer, in sickness and in health, to love and cherish until death do you part?'

The unspoken words rang in my ears, and I sat up quickly.

'No, no, no! Impossible!'

These words I spoke aloud and my voice echoed around the large room and disappeared into the shadows. I pulled my hair back and held it bunched in my hand for a moment, tugging at it to drag me back to reality. Then I jumped out of bed, ran to the window and flung the shutters open. Sunlight flooded in, momentarily blinding me, and I felt the strength of its warmth on the front of my body. I stepped out onto the small balcony and stood still, breathing in the light perfume of the wisteria that rambled around the railing. Then I focussed and looked across the terracotta rooftops to the distant blue outline of the Sibillini mountains. This was Macerata in the warm heart of Italy, this was my new life.

1

'Where do you live?' I smothered a yawn, and my eyes watered slightly as I looked at the student in front of me. His dark Italian face was heavy with concentration as he forced his beautiful curving lips to shape the awkward Anglo-Saxon sounds.

'I live at Macerata!' He replied carefully, *'La più bella città del mondo.'*

He raised his arm in a gesture of proud triumph and turned to receive the acclaim of the other students. He was Caesar greeting his countrymen.

I sighed and glanced down at my small gold wristwatch and my heart missed a beat as I remembered Hugh giving it to me on my twenty-first birthday. There was something touchingly old-fashioned about dear Hughie. The small gold hands on the mother of pearl face delicately pointed to four fifty-five. I stifled another yawn, relieved to find only five minutes left of the lesson. So, Flavio Marcello thought Macerata the most beautiful city in the world? I decided against asking the unkind question that sprang to my mind. Had Flavio ever been to another city? Time was fortunately too short.

'I live in Macerata, Flavio - in, in!' I repeated the small word 'in' with too much force. Flavio's arms dropped to his sides and remained momentarily still. His face fell into gloomy blackness, and then he looked at me. His eyes told me more than I wanted to know about myself. I felt the colour rush to my pale English cheeks as I read his Latin thoughts. Was I really so dull, so academic, so lacking in human joy?

'I live IN Macerata - in, in!' Flavio repeated my words, perfectly mimicking the shrill tone of my voice and my clipped educated accent. The whole class laughed, and one girl, the small dark sullen-faced girl who always sat next to Flavio, clapped her hands. Flavio's arms were flying again, fanning the sound of laughter. He was Pavarotti receiving applause.

I almost laughed aloud and then added in a different, softer tone, attempting to bring the room back to order.

'Enough - *basta*! The lesson is over! Remember to prepare the vocabulary on page six for tomorrow's conversation.'

Before I had finished speaking, the students were making for the door. Flavio was surrounded by a group of friends as they began to leave the room. I hastily pushed my books into my old leather briefcase and then glanced up, just as Flavio looked back at me from the doorway. His raised his hand, almost in benefaction, and flashed me a smile. He was the Pope advertising toothpaste.
I lifted my own hand in reply, but Flavio had already dodged out of the door frame and disappeared with his entourage. The room became silent and leaden with the sultry heat of the afternoon.

Half an hour later, I was sitting under a parasol on the terrace of my favourite café, slowly eating a pistachio ice-cream. The moment was luxurious but lonely. My daily life was punctuated with such small treats and consolations. The sweet, nutty ice cream melted in my mouth as I thought that, after all, I had never wanted to be a teacher. I had been wandering through the University hall when I had noticed the job application on the notice board and, somehow, it had called out to me. My only friend in Macerata, Francesca, had gone to Paris for three months, and I had begun to wonder just why I was living in the city. A lovely place but possibly not *la più bella città del mondo*. It had been so different when I had taken my exchange months here as a student. Then I had been part of the life, but now, although I had enrolled in a part-time postgraduate course, I was... well, older if not wiser. Why I had thought teaching English would introduce me to a broader circle of people now seemed ridiculous. I was *'la professoressa inglese'* and thus set apart.

    I carefully spooned up the last mouthful of the melted, smooth green ice-cream and then dabbed my lips delicately with the small paper napkin. My every movement felt constrained, and I held my arms close to my sides as though I was in a room packed with people. I took a deep breath, trying to dismiss my loneliness and the feeling that I was horribly out of place. The waiter came to take my money and clear the table. He smiled down at me, a friendly avuncular smile.

    'You like the pistachio, is very good, no… is the best in Macerata?' He was just making conversation and I sensed pity in his voice. I looked up at him as he clutched his tray to his heart and glowed with self-satisfaction. He spoke better English than Flavio, I thought, with a sense of hopelessness. No, I had never ever wanted to be a teacher.

'*Si, grazie.*' I replied in a small, polite voice before hurrying away from the café, away from his sympathy, his cheery benevolence. Why did Italians have to be so enthusiastic? Suddenly I longed for the cynical, coldness of the English. Why couldn't the waiter just slam down the bill and morosely wait for the money and a tip? All this ardent, gushing fervour just exhausted and annoyed me. It was too hot.

I sauntered through the shade of the loggia, the weight of my briefcase heavy in my hand. As I rounded the corner, I saw Flavio and his friends ahead of me. They were talking or maybe arguing as they walked. Flavio was in the centre and, as usual, his arms flailing wildly in the air as he held court. I looked at his strong shoulders and small waist and felt a shiver of desire. As though with some animal sense, he turned immediately and looked into my eyes. I felt my English cheeks flush again as I smiled at him. Flavio raised his arm and beckoned me towards him, opening and closing his fingers. He was a father beckoning to his child.

I felt the magnetic pull of his charm and slowly moved forward.

'*Ciao, Professoressa, ciao*!' Flavio called out to me, and I stopped still for a moment, then gave a small nod of acknowledgement and walked in the opposite direction.

My heart thudded in my ears as I crossed the piazza in the blinding heat of the sun. What was I thinking? Flavio was my student. How could I let myself think of him in any other way? But my heart thumped louder in my ears as I imagined his waving arms closing around me. I reached the other side of the piazza and then suddenly tripped on the kerb, sharply twisting my ankle. My briefcase flew from my hot, slippery hand and slid across the pavement, bursting open and strewing my books in the dust. I blinked away tears of pain and defeat as I knelt on the dusty cobbles. An arm came round my shoulders, and a figure blotted out the sun. A small sob escaped me as I allowed myself to sink into the man's strength. Flavio had come to my rescue.

'Hold on, you've broken the strap on your sandal. Just stay still a moment, and I'll collect your books.'

A quiet, English voice spoke softly in my ear. Not Flavio then.

Five minutes later, I was sitting in another café with an ice-cold cloth napkin wrapped around my ankle. My books had been carefully replaced in my briefcase and the broken strap of my sandal temporarily tied. I looked with gratitude at the man sitting beside me. He was sipping a small, dark espresso in silence, an enigmatic smile played around his lips as though he were thinking of something slightly amusing.

'Thank you so much for your kindness' I said quietly.

'No trouble at all.'

The man's short answer pleased me, as did the dismissive gesture he made, his thin hand momentarily brushing the air. I looked at his elegantly creased, pale grey, linen suit and his Panama hat placed on the empty chair between us. He was so very English that I thought we might begin to converse about the weather. In fact, he was almost too English to be English and here was something too romantic about him. I wondered if he was a gigolo or some sophisticated type of tourist guide. I decided to attempt a question, glad to speak English, I said slowly,

'Are you on holiday here?'

'No, I live in Macerata. My name is Jago Bradshaw.'

He held out his hand, and I shivered slightly as his cool, smooth hand enclose mine in a formal handshake. Jago, of course, he would be called Jago, a name straight from a romantic novel. Soon we would be dancing in the Millish Boon moonlight. I stopped my random thoughts as I realised he was still talking in that low, calm voice,

'And you? What are you doing here?'

Struggling to appear equally calm, I took a deep breath and replied,

'My name is Verity, Verity Gresham. I teach English - just beginners.'

'Ah - of course, your briefcase of books. I should have guessed you were a teacher. Verity... hmm such a truly English name.' He seemed annoyingly satisfied with my reply, and added, 'I'm the Professor in residence at the University here. I haven't seen you around before, but I stay mainly in the research department. Have you been here long?'

'No, only two months.' I glanced quickly up at him, thinking not a gigolo or tourist guide then, and almost giggled. He was reading the menu, and suddenly he looked at me over the edge of it, his eyes dark grey and direct,

'Would you care for an ice-cream... or maybe a coffee... a cup of tea?'

I enjoyed his quiet sophistication and the low timbre of his voice, almost a drawl. I particularly liked his deep-set eyes under his straight dark eyebrows. He seemed to be looking through me, and I felt my throat tighten with something like excitement... or maybe fear? Was he a parody of the educated Englishman abroad? Was he even telling the truth about his work at the University? I had never seen him there.

'Actually, I'd just eaten an ice-cream before I fell over....' I replied, then added quickly 'but I'd love a coffee.'

I was now annoyed with myself as I realised I was anxious for our time together not to come to an end.

The man, this Jago, raised his hand in a simple, commanding manner, and the waiter immediately came to his side. I relaxed into my chair and felt the ease of childhood slip over me like a soft mantle. I gave myself up to him, happy to be in his charge and suppressed any lingering doubts I felt.

2

I awoke the next morning, in my bed under the dancing cherubs. I stretched and sighed as the memory of the day before flickered into my head. I closed my eyes and let my personal video play behind my lids. Jago paying the waiter, summoning a taxi and insisting I should go to his doctor's to have my ankle checked. The scene changed, now, inside the taxi, I was hotly aware of Jago's nearness in the cool air-conditioned car and, again, a flicker of excitement mixed with fear.

I opened my eyes and smiled up at one of the cherubs who had become my little favourite. He held a small golden bow and arrow and was cheekily aiming at the rounded pink bottom of another baby angel.

I smiled because my fear had been so needless. The taxi driver had taken us across the city and stopped outside a respectable doctor's surgery. I had not been abducted, on the contrary, Jago had told the taxi to wait as he half-carried me into the waiting room. I was beginning to feel a fraud as my ankle hardly hurt. Was I abducting Jago in some complicated way? Leading him on? I definitely wanted to spend more time with him, and when the doctor gravely diagnosed nothing more than a slight sprain, I sighed, apologised and hobbled out of the room. I was worried about the taxi waiting. Where I had grown up in Newmarket, taxis were a constant bright yellow and black presence in the town, rushing back and forth to the racecourses and the station, but seldom used by my family. To keep one waiting, ticking over in the heat of the Italian sun seemed unthinkable. Jago, apparently, had no such thought in his head as he opened the rear door for me and I slipped into the chilled Mercedes luxury. We sat for a moment in silence then, to my surprise and delight, Jago had suggested an outing.

'Not much you can do today on that foot. How about resting it up? Have you ever been to the hill village of Monte San Martino? There are a few hours before sunset, and it's a beautiful place to watch the sun go down?'

He spoke casually, and I nodded, trying to stay equally cool although my stomach was clenched with excitement. Before I could say a word, Jago took my nod for agreement and gave directions to the taxi driver. By silently nodding, I had avoided the truth. I had been to Monte San Martino before when I was a student, but now, well now, I just didn't mention it. A sin by omission? For some reason, almost unknown to myself, I decided to let Jago now play the part of tour guide. A handsome, sophisticated tour guide. As we set off, Jago insisted that I sit sideways across the back seat with my foot resting on his knees. Did he lay his hands on my ankles or further up my legs? No, not for a moment. Had I wanted him to?

I abruptly cut the film strip playing in my head and frowned up at my cherub as I thought about my own question. It was impossible to answer. I had, but there again, I hadn't. There would have been something disappointingly cheesy in the laying on of hands. I turned on my side and curled up in a tight ball as I reflected on the wonderful peace of the taxi ride into the mountains. The cool conditioned air, the slow, stately driving... no screeching tyres around the hairpin bends... and the low voice of Jago talking about mediaeval art. It had been more seductive than a stolen kiss.

When we arrived in the small piazza of the village, I was carefully deposited on the cobbles and helped to limp to a small bar under a loggia. Here I had been surprised to find that Jago was well known... well known in the way that everyone danced around him, almost bowing and scraping. He spoke impeccable Italian and chatted to the barman and the few people sitting in the bar. Maybe chatted is the wrong word. He had enquired gently about their health and that of their families... much as a visiting king might ask after his people.

I rolled over onto my back and yawned, even my favourite cherub looked frustrated by my dreaming. It was nearly time to get up and be ready for another day of teaching. I yawned again and wiggled my foot and allowed myself the little luxury of staying stretched out on the bed for a moment longer. Just long enough to remember the visit we had tried to make to the tiny chapel perched on the edge of the village ramparts. Jago had knocked on the priest's door, but there had been no answer. He had looked at me with his dark, severe grey eyes as he apologised for this disappointment. He told me of the masterpiece, the Crivelli triptych that hung inside. Did I confess, then, that I had already seen it? That I had been to the village with a group of my student friends? No, I just accepted his invitation to dine in a restaurant where we could watch the sun sink behind the Sibillini mountains. Certainly, a restaurant far too expensive for me in my student days. There would be no cause for more omissions, and I smiled in agreement when Jago suggested we tried another time and that he would arrange it correctly. Had he held my hand over the candlelit table as the sky blushed? No, but I had wanted him to. And still, the taxi had waited.

But today was a new day, and now, it was absolutely time to arise, shower and stop dreaming like a romantic heroine in a Jane Austen novel.

But when I looked in the mirror over the washbasin in the bathroom, I saw I was smiling in a simpering Victorian way.

3

Another hot day in my classroom stretched ahead of me. The first few groups were industrious and stretched my limited ability. I even enjoyed the challenge, and the time passed quickly enough. After lunch, always a sleep-inducing exercise even though I only ate a salad and never drank wine, I sat again in my favourite café, under the same parasol and slowly sipped an espresso. Today there was a different waiter, and I found I now missed the friendly smile of the other. I tried to make my coffee last as long as possible as the long lunch break stretched ahead. I read my book and tried not to think about taking another coffee in the piazza where I had sat with Jago. I was reading Sense and Sensibility, not for the first time, and the words blurred on the page. I considered going back to my apartment for a short siesta but my ankle, though hardly painful as I sat down, was not quite ready for extra cobblestones. I looked down at it and saw no swelling, not even a bruise beginning to show. I was wearing what my mother called 'sensible shoes' and what I preferred to call loafers. My small amount of fashion sense had then made me choose to wear my close-fitting Capri jeans rather than a thin summery dress and now, not surprisingly, I felt too hot. I noticed that the skin of my pale English arms was starting to tan, which was most surprising as I always sat in the shade.

I closed my book and looked under the edge of the dark blue umbrella and up at the cloudless sky.

Italy was full of life surprises, which is probably why I had fled here after my disastrous non-wedding. Poor Hughie, how I had hurt him. My eyes filled with annoying tears as I thought how I had destroyed all our plans for a life together. I blinked rapidly, not allowing the tears time to fall and then started with alarm as my mobile rang from deep inside my bag. I scrambled to find it, saw the light flashing, grabbed at it and tried to press the green spot... without success. It gave its last ring and died into blackness in my hand. I tapped at it angrily, searching for the last call number and saw Hugh's name. I drew in my breath sharply... had he known I was thinking of him? I shook my head in annoyance at my own stupidity. I thought for a long moment about returning his call or taking the radical step of blocking his number. Then, with a heavy sigh, I simply turned off my phone and slipped it back into the depths of my bag. There it rested, hidden between files and textbooks and all the clutter of my new life.

    I downed the last bitter drop of my coffee and left the payment in a small saucer. I stood up, testing my ankle and decided to stroll to the park in my sensible shoes. I made my way slowly through the shady loggia and toward the park, carefully avoiding the main piazza where Jago might well be taking an elegant postprandial coffee. He had taken my phone number, and he was hardly the type to lose it, so I was determined to wait for his call and not to seek him out. I soon reached the fountain in the park and sat down in the shade. The air was cooled by the sprinkling water, and the occasional breeze blew across my face. I opened my book again and began to read.

"... therefore, I have had to oppose, by endeavouring to appear indifferent where I have been most deeply interested..."

The stylish phrasing reached out to me, causing me to smile with pleasure. Austen, as usual, had spoken directly into my modern-day mood. Then my smile turned to a frown as I self-confessed that I had been hoping it was Jago calling into my bag. Poor Hughie, I sighed as I thought about it and closed the book once more. I took out my pen and notebook planning to draft out a letter. Hugh deserved more than my departing hurried and tearful attempt to explain my change of heart. My pen hovered over the thick cream paper of my lovely blank moleskin notebook. I began to write, but it did not start "Dear Hughie." For some time now, I had been playing with the idea of writing a novel. Suddenly, the words were dripping inkily from my pen, flowing in a fast torrent.

4

Genevieve walked down the garden path that led to the river, brushing her fingers lightly through the dewy lavender. The sweet perfume rose into the air around her and she breathed in, smiled and then frowned. The small crease that appeared between her perfect arched brows did nothing to mar her beauty.

'How dare he be late?'

She muttered the words under her breath as she idly kicked her silver sandals through the gravel on the path. Angrily she snapped a long stem of lavender and threaded it into her pale blonde hair as she carried on downhill until she reached the river bank. It was June and the insects had not quite begun their summer work, zooming back and forth over the water. The afternoon was perfect, or it should have been, but Rory was late and Genevieve was in a very bad mood.

'I shall never speak to him again.' Now she spoke aloud, and she jumped as a man's voice answered,

'Quite right, speak to me instead.'

Genevieve looked around nervously and then said in a high-pitched furious voice, her temper rising higher,

'I don't know where you are, or who you are but this is private land.'

'But I'm not on the land.' There was the slapping sound of oars as a small rowing boat pulled out from the willows that edged the river.

'Even you, my beauty, can't own the flowing water.'

Genevieve hesitated a moment, taking in the bare broad chest of the man and the movement of his muscular shoulders as he dabbed the oars into the water, holding the boat still and now very near to her. Recovering her equilibrium with a quick shake of her head, she said angrily,

'I believe we do, in fact, own this side of the river, halfway across.'

To her further annoyance, the young man threw back his head and roared with laughter. Now she noticed his strong neck and how his Adam's apple throbbed in his throat. He was possibly, no definitely, the most handsome man she had ever seen. She felt suddenly too warm, her skin damp under her long hair. She shook her head again and the sprig of lavender fell, wafted in the air for a moment and then dropped into the water. The man deftly dipped his hand into the flow, caught the lavender and held it out to her, smiling wickedly.

'Do you want it back, my beauty?'

Instinctively, she reached out her hand to take it from him, wondering at the same time why she was doing so. Just as she was about to take it, he pulled it away and she fell forward. In an instant, he stood up, his feet planted firmly apart, balancing easily as he circled her in his arms and drew her into the boat. He placed her carefully on the narrow wooden seat and looked down at her, still smiling.

'Are you all right? The bank is slippery with last night's rain. But I saved you from a dunking.'

'It was all your fault. I was just about to...'

'Kiss me?'

He sat down facing her and the small boat rocked gently for a moment, then he reached for the oars and edged the boat back into the shade of the overhanging willows. Genevieve watched in silence as he swung the blades of the oars above the water, the sunlight sparkling momentarily on the bright droplets. Still remaining quiet and transfixed, feeling a strange inevitability in the scene, Genevieve waited, without moving, as he swivelled the oars in the rowlocks and then carefully, without dampening her dress which spread out around her, he rested the oars into the boat. She watched, fascinated, as his long fingers deftly tied the boat to the arching trunk of the tree. She was mesmerised by his confidence and the two short words that seemed to hang in the warm air around them.

'Kiss me.'

Then, she bit her lip and decided it was time, high time, to pull herself together. She pushed aside some soft willow leaves that brushed her hair and said,

'I don't know who you are or...'

'Apologies, my name is Jago, Jago Bradshaw and I live just upriver, nearer to Henley and on the opposite bank. I own the other half of the river, I imagine. And you are...?'

'I'm Genevieve Hurley and, well, I live here...' She had intended to sound angry, but her voice was breathless and suddenly he ducked his head and kissed her very lightly on the cheek, then said in a low husky voice,

'Another apology, but I just couldn't help it. I wanted to kiss you from the moment I saw you sulking so prettily in your garden.'

Genevieve raised her hand to her cheek, feeling the imprint of his lips and with some idea of holding on to the sensation. She knew she should be angry, even insulted... but now she was tired of anger. She reached out her hand and slipped it around the back of his head, running her fingers through his long dark hair and pulled him to her. They kissed, hard, mouth to mouth with their lips closed. She heard him draw in his breath sharply and she almost laughed, but now his tongue was pressing her lips apart and she ran her hand down the length of his spine. He pulled her against him and they fell back together onto the planks of the boat. Never had she felt such a rush of desire and her fingers were fumbling to open the top button of his jeans before he had even slipped his hand up her skirt. Then they were both panting and tearing at each other clothes as the boat rocked gently and then faster in the water.

I looked at my watch and gasped, then ran my pen angrily through the few pages I had written, scribbling zig-zag through the inky black words. 'Utter rubbish!' I muttered as angrily as my created Genevieve, and snapped the book shut, not waiting for the ink to dry. Then grabbing my bag, I hobbled quickly back into town.

5

I had very nearly been late, and I am never late, I hate lateness. Some of the students were already in the room when I arrived, not quite breathless but flustered. I sat quickly at my desk and pulled out my files and a textbook and laid them neatly in front of me. I pushed my black Moleskin notebook into the bottom of my bag as though to punish it for causing me to be late, nearly late. I glanced up at the wall clock and saw the large hand tick over onto the hour. I clapped my hands, and a small group of students stopped chatting together and slowly took their seats without any enthusiasm. I smothered a sigh in sympathy. If they were reluctant to learn, then I could match that with my own disinclination to impart the joys of the English language. This class, only half-full this afternoon, was definitely my hardest challenge, and I was not particularly interested in rising to it. They were here because they needed to pass the basic English exam to further their University courses... future biochemists, surveyors, lawyers, dentists, a few engineers and sundry others that I had not bothered to ask. Not one of them showed a glimmer of interest in any language other than their own. I smothered another sigh, almost a yawn as I thought how I had not been born to be a teacher. My own presence in the room was not due to high principles... more to earn enough money, in a pleasant and easy enough way, to fund my escapee life. I flicked my hair back behind my ears and opened the textbook,

'Good afternoon, everybody.' I spoke firmly and listened to their sing-song response. At least, I thought to myself, I had taught them two useful words. I continued resolutely,

'Please turn to page fifteen.' At this small command, there was the usual shuffling of bodies as they regrouped, most of them having forgotten their books and all of them struggling to work out the page number. I clapped my hands and tried another tack,

'First, count with me. One two...' I counted on slowly, clapping between each number, and this they enjoyed. Their young adult faces becoming childlike as they looked up at me, smiling with delight. This, they could do. Just as I reached the number fourteen, the door burst open and in swept Flavio, followed by his usual gang. I stopped counting and glared at him,

'You are very late, Flavio.'

'*Sono molto dispiace, Professoressa, ma...*'

'Stop!' I held up my hand and said in an ice-cold voice, 'If you are going to apologise, then speak English.'

Flavio clasping his hands together in front of him, a penitent praying and beseeching absolution.

'Sorry, excuse me, I late for no thing.'

I scowled at him and said, 'Please take your seat, and your friends, too. Quickly, now, and find page fifteen in the textbook. You have interrupted my lesson.'

Flavio gave a flourishing bow and then vaulted over two desks and landed into a seat. Now, there was general laughter and some applause at his athletic move. His friends settled around him and the sulky girl I had noticed before, quickly took out her textbook, glowered at me and then shared it with Flavio. I turned my back on the class and wrote 'PAGE FIFTEEN' in large chalky capitals and then, in my own neat handwriting, 'Please excuse me for being late. I shall be on time in the future.'

I took a deep breath and turned back to face the students. Some of them sat with books open now, others sprawled lazily, chatting idly or listening to Flavio. I just made out some of his words '...*più bella quando arrabbiata... su questo non ci piove... bellissima!*' This was followed by a gust of laughter from his admirers, only the dark-faced girl frowned and bit her lip. I felt the colour rush to my cheeks as I realised he was saying that I was more beautiful when I was angry, *bellissima*... very beautiful. His words confused me for a moment, and I turned back to the blackboard and continued to write, noticing that my hand was shaking slightly. Should I respond, call order, demand another apology? I began to write a list of nouns with the sound 'ough' as I considered the matter. through, though, bought, cough….enough. I wrote steadily now as I took another deep breath and I tried not to think that I liked him saying I was beautiful, *bellissima*. Was he, even now, appreciating the rearview of my tight-fitting Capri jeans? The chalk snapped into two and flicked across the floor. In a lightning move, Flavio was out of his seat and picking up the two pieces. He held them out to me, cupping them in the palm of his olive-skinned hand as he very slowly said,

'Please excuse me for being late. I shall be on time in the future.'

He was reading from the blackboard, of course, and his accent was appalling but, oh, his dark brown eyes looked into my soul and the brush of his fingers on mine as he passed me the chalk sent a shiver down my spine... and then to some inner central part of my body. I squared my shoulders and dragged my eyes away from him and said,

'Thank you, Flavio...' I tried to ignore the little bow he gave to me, but I turned to him again and saw how his dark curls fell forward over his forehead. Standing very upright for a moment, he looked at me again, now there was laughter shining from under his dark sooty lashes. Then, he spun on his Italian leather heel and went quietly back to his seat. Only for a second did I allow myself to admire his rearview. I added calmly,

'Now, perhaps, we can begin?'

6

The lesson had dragged on, the oppressive heat of the afternoon spreading a cloud of lethargy. I tried, not very hard, but I finally managed to liven the group up by allowing them to lead me astray and into their interest in retro British pop music. Not being my field of expertise, I listened to their iPhones squeakily singing popular songs and managed to translate some of the lines. The word 'love' came up frequently, and inevitably, some of the words were crude slang. I compromised and gave some watered down translations of the lyrics. At least, I had opened a vein of interest in the English language and decided I would tap into it. I left them with homework, and for once, they were enthusiastic. I scrubbed out my earlier writing, demanding an apology for lateness and the cruelly irregular us of the 'ow' sound, and wrote instead,

'Find three lines from a British 60's pop song that you don't understand. Write them down and bring them to my next lesson.'

There was a slow buzz of excitement in the room as they slowly translated my chalky writing.

When the final bell rang at five-thirty, I was amazed to see them still tapping the question into their phones and not rushing for the door. Flavio was in the middle of his group, fielding their questions. I decided to leave them to it and collected my work together and made for the door. Just as I reached it,

Flavio, in another of his rapid moves, stood in my way and then turned and opened the door for me,

'Good Evening, Professoressa Gresham,' he spoke softly and then, as though he could contain his Italian no longer, he added in almost a querying way, *'Passa una bella serata?'*

I nodded quickly as I passed close by him, close enough to breathe in the perfume of his warm skin. A fragrant combination of something that reminded me of wild herbs and sunshine. As I walked away from the classroom, I was sorely tempted to turn around to see if he was watching me. But, I walked on, my reliable loafers making no noise on the highly polished floor and wondering why this young man made my heart thump loudly in my ears. *Una bella serata?* I repeated the words to myself as I emerged into the late afternoon sunshine outside the University portal. Would I have a beautiful evening? It didn't seem very likely. A pleasant evening was as much as I could hope for. I wended my way slowly back to my apartment, feeling lonely and tired and wondering why I was here in Macerata. On the way, I stopped at a few shops and bought provisions for my not-to-be *bellissima* evening. A ripe melon, some cheeses, figs and a few oranges were to be my companions... and a bottle of the local Verdicchio would help.

I climbed the winding stone staircase and had nearly reached the top landing and my front door when a voice called up to me,

'Signorina, Signorina Verità. Ho un messaggio per te!'

I turned and went down to the landing where my landlady was standing, holding out an envelope. She tended to hijack all the post I received and then hold onto it, hoping I would share any news. Not that I received much post. My mother's letters, mostly, and occasionally a postcard from a travelling friend. Hugh and all my friends used text messages. I attempted to take the envelope, but my landlady held onto it, saying,

'Non è una lettera dall'Inghilterra.'

I tugged the letter from her hand, thanked her and slipped it in my bag and made to climb the stairs again. I heard her disappointed sigh, followed by a few unintelligible grumbles and I called down,

'Vorresti un bicchiere di vino, Signora Brindisi? Fra dieci minuti?'

An enthusiastic string of *'si, si si, volentieri …'* came up to me from below in answer to my invitation, and I thought how she was possibly even lonelier than me.

I hurriedly unlocked my door and pulled out the thick cream envelope and examined the precise hand-written black lettering with just my name... no postage stamp or return address on the back. I ripped it open and read,

Dear Verity,

I hope you will forgive my addressing you with your first name, but Miss Gresham feels too formal after the pleasant evening we spent together in Monte San Martino.

I called on you earlier in the hope of finding you at home, but I am now writing this quick note and leaving it with Signora Brindisi. I am confident she will make sure you receive it, but maybe not in time to meet my request to meet you this evening. I have contacted the priest at the chapel in Monte San Martino, and we could view the Crivelli at eight o'clock this evening if you happen to be free. Perhaps we could also have dinner together again, too?

If you should receive this in time, please call my mobile or leave a message. I shall drive into the piazza near your home at a quarter past seven in the hope of finding you agreeable to the outing.

Yours sincerely,
Jago Bradshaw.

I read the letter twice and then once again, amused at the formal, somewhat archaic structure of what he called a 'quick note'. I smiled, wondering how long he could make a letter. Then, I looked at my phone and saw it was nearly six-fifteen and Signora Brindisi would be on her way up to share my Verdicchio. Next, I looked in the mirror. My face was pink from the heat and some effect of the sunshine from my picnic lunch in the park. My auburn hair, usually reasonably smooth, was frizzing slightly. I needed a shower and... what to wear? Because, of course, I was most agreeable to the outing and sent a very brief text message in acceptance. Luckily I had bought the Verdicchio from the chilled shelf of the Pinacoteca, and now I pulled the cork and took two glasses out onto the small balcony that hung off my small living room. Then, tipping a few olives into a bowl, I added them to my preparation. I was just wondering how long Signora Brindisi would expect to stay for her aperitif when there was a knock on the door.

    I went to open it quickly, and there stood Signora Brindisi, beaming with happiness and brandishing a plate of thinly sliced Gran Padano cheese. I ushered her in, and she looked around curiously, inspecting, I assumed, what I had done to the apartment since I had taken up residence. I looked anxiously at the poster of a Giacometti drawing that I had blu-tacked onto the wall above my little dining table, but she clasped her hands together in approval. Relieved, I ushered her out onto the balcony, and we sat together, sipping the crisp, dry wine. In less than five minutes she had me telling her all about Jago Bradshaw and his invitation. In another twenty minutes, halfway through the bottle of wine, she made me take a shower while she ironed my favourite white linen shirt.

    At seven-fifteen, she was pushing me through my front door and hurrying me down the stairs and out into the evening sunshine. I turned to her as I left to thank her, but she waved me away, flapping her hands as she called after me.

    'Passa una bella serata! Vai! Divertiti!'

I rounded the corner into the piazza and saw a pale blue Alfa Romeo waiting. Hmm, I thought to myself, at least there was now a chance of a beautiful evening and possibly some divertiti-ish diverting fun, too.

7

The sun was already slipping behind the hazy blue Sibillini mountains as we drove out of the city toward Monte San Martino. Jago had, just for one moment, lost some of his usual calm composure as he had seen me come into the piazza. He had leapt out of the car and hurriedly opened the passenger door for me, stammered a greeting in both English and Italian and then fell silent, a streak of colour across his high cheekbones. But now, with a Mozart clarinet concerto playing in the background, he was back in control.

'Very glad you could come, Verity,' he said over the music, the noise of the engine and the rushing wind. 'Such a perfect evening for a drive into the country.'

Somehow he made it sound like an outing to the Cotswolds, but maybe that was just the very Englishness of his voice. I nodded and smiled, but couldn't help thinking that the spectacular mountain range spread out in front of us, glowing in the sunset, somehow deserved more.

'It's spectacular, I love the Sibillini!'

Now he nodded and smiled, and I realised I hadn't done much better. My voice had a childish ring to it as I raised it to make myself heard. Then, for the next few miles, we remained in silence, not particularly awkward but definitely not comfortable. I decided I should make more effort and, as we neared a small town, I said,

'This is Sarnano Terme, isn't it? I remember ski-ing up in the mountains above here when I was at the University as a student.'

Now, Jago gave me a fleeting sideways glance and said, 'Really, you were a student here?'

'Yes, a few years ago, now. Only for one term as I was on the Erasmus exchange scheme.'

'Really, I see. Must have been before I began my research here. I'm sure I would have remembered you.'

I was pleased with this subtle compliment and said,

'That's why I came back here. I liked it so much, and I made a very good friend here. And you, how did you choose to work at the University in Macerata?'

Now I looked sideways at Jago and was in time to see him frown, almost wince. He ignored my question and replied,

'You are so young... a teacher hardly older than your students.'

'True.' I laughed, 'I'm not sure that some of them aren't actually older than I am.'

'But not as old as me, surely.'

He gave a small laugh, and I thought it better to change the subject. We had passed through the small town of Sarnano Terme, and now the road was weaving along a valley. Then, as we rounded a long bend, the hilltop village of Monte San Martino came into view, perched high on a craggy outcrop of rock and glowing pink in the last of the sunlight.

'It's so beautiful, isn't it?' Now, I was back to my squeaky schoolgirl voice, and I began to despair that I would be able to make any intelligent conversation all evening. My *bella serata* was not going too well so far.

Jago drove around the small road that clung to the village walls and pulled to a halt outside the chapel. As the engine ticked into silence, he turned to me,

'I'll just go to the priest's house and get the key. Won't be a minute.'

I watched him stroll across the cobbled road and knock on a cottage door. He stood waiting, his hands linked loosely behind his back, his head bowed, quiet, elegant and ... how old? Surely not more than forty? Did it matter? I pulled down the sun-visor and flicked open the mirror. I examined myself critically. My hair had dried in the breeze of our journey in the open car and I attempted to smooth it down. A hopeless task. My skin, usually so pale, was pleasingly tinged with a light tan. That was good. My green eyes peered back at me, questioning. How did I come to be sitting in an Alfa Romeo outside a village priest's house? I smiled at my own answer. Why not? This was my new life in Italy, a diverting diversion from my life in Suffolk. With one last effort to push my long hair back behind my ears, I closed the mirror and looked through the windscreen. Now, only a small red-gold arc of the sun showed above the lowest dip between the mountains. I stared at it, my eyes blurring, and at that moment, Jago returned to the car.

'I have the key, shall we?'

He opened the car door, and I slipped out hurriedly and saw a small man waiting by the chapel entrance. Still dazzled by the sun, I blinked in surprise. Was it Mussolini or Picasso in a priest's dark robes? And was he holding a dinner fork in his hand rather than a key? I blinked again, rapidly, and dismissed the surreal image as Jago ushered me toward the chapel. Ushered? Somehow the word fitted as he moved me forward with an arm hovering a few inches from my back, no actual body contact made.

'*Buona sera, Signorina. Benvenuti!*'

Now that the priest was in focus, I realised that my first impression had not been so wrong. He had the stature of Mussolini and the glowing brown eyes of Picasso... and he was brandishing a fork in his left hand. I shook his right hand and made the appropriate response of greeting and gratitude, and then he said,

'*Per favore, Signorina*, we speak English, no?' He nodded eagerly, 'Is for me a rare pleasure.'

'Of course.' I nodded, and before I could say more, he added,

'Last time I speak the English it was with *Principe Carlo d'Inghilterra, si, si* your Princy Charlie. *Si, si... ma... vieni, vieni dentro.*'

He held out his short arm, brandishing the fork and welcomed me into the chapel. I passed in front of him, feeling awkwardly tall and very aware of his garlicky breath. Jago followed me closely, again his arm around me but not touching. The chapel was dark, and I hesitated, causing Jago to collide with me. He stepped back immediately and apologised, saying,

'It takes a while to accustom to the dark. Benito, have you turned off the alarm?'

Had he really called the priest Benito? And just what was that about Prince Charles? Carlo? Wasn't that the name of the Crivelli brother, the painter? I suppressed a ripple of laughter rising up inside me at the farcical scenario I had entered. Then the priest almost pushed past me and said,

'*Dio Mio, no... l'allarme antifurto! Certo*, I must turn off 'ere.'

He stood on a rickety wooden bench, reached above his head and flicked what looked like an ordinary electric switch, Well, ordinary for Italy in the 1950s, maybe. Then, tapping the side of his stubby nose and winking, he turned to me,

'Iago always remember to tell me. Is important secret alarm for the Crivelli. *Securità, no?*'

I nodded in agreement although I thought of the only other Crivelli masterpieces I had ever seen, hanging in the National Gallery, and wondered if the security measure quite matched. But I was distracted by Benito's soft pronunciation of the letter J. It changed the name completely. Jago rang of a romantic hero in a lightweight novel but Iago? Hmm, Shakespeare's most sinister villain, the evil manipulator and liar. Did Iago... as Benito pronounced it ... eeeyahgo... suit my gallant escort better than Jago? I remained lost in my stream of thoughts as we walked slowly up the aisle between the few rows of rush-seated chairs. With a jolt like an electric shock, I realised it should soon have been my wedding day. I would have been walking up the long aisle of the ancient cathedral in Bury St Edmunds, my ivory silk dress flowing behind me, my arm resting on my father as he led me toward dear Hughie. I felt dizzy at the idea, and again the question rose up... what was I doing here? What on earth was I doing in a small chapel with a fork-wielding priest and my unknown Jago-Iago? Then Jago's voice broke into my reverie, and I realised I was standing close to the Crivelli polyptych.

'It's truly wonderful, isn't it?' Now Jago's voice was breathless with wonder, almost as childlike as mine had been earlier in our *bella serata* together. I let the brilliant colours of the painting soothe me for a moment, and then I turned to Jago and saw that his face was lit with passion. I rested my hand on his arm and said,

'Thank you, thank you so much for bringing me here. It is truly beautiful.'

He rested his hand over mine and nodded but said nothing. We stood close together absorbed in the majestic solemnity of the masterpiece, the reds and greens shimmering between the dark gold.

Then the voice of the priest broke the awed silence,

'Now, now you see the hand of Principe Carlo. *Vieni, vieni!*'

I turned reluctantly away from the glowing painting and saw that Benito was already standing by the door. Prince Charles' hand? Was I to be shown some weird relic? Was this to be another surreal moment of the *bella serata*? I heard Jago sigh, and as I walked back down the aisle, he hovered after me like a respectful uncle. The brief moment of intimacy had passed, and I wondered if it would return. But, Benito was waiting, his face now alight with excitement as he carefully opened a book-marked page in a large leather-covered book. I realised it was a visitor's book and there, inkily alone on an otherwise blank page was the royal signature.

'Goodness!' I said in surprise, 'You had a visit from Prince Charles?'

Benito nodded his eyes filled with tears as he replaced a fluttery piece of cream tissue paper over the page.

'Yes, Prince Charles, here. He stand here where you stand.' He pointed down to the stone floor beneath my feet, and for a second, I wondered if I should move. But Benito continued, 'He very experto on art of Crivelli, he know very much. Very big scholar. Like Iago, my good friend Iago.'

Overcome with emotion, he suddenly clasped his arms around Jago. The difference in their stature made it easy for Jago to look at me over the bald tonsured head of the priest and raise his eyebrows as he endured the embrace for a long moment. Then, smiling at me, a genuine wide smile of real amusement, he patted Benito's back and edged away. We all moved awkwardly toward the door.

'Shall I turn on the alarm again, Benito?' Jago asked as Benito was already outside.

'*Si, si, dio mio*! Always I forget. Grazie, Iago, *grazie mille*.' He slapped his hand to his forehead and waved the fork with his other hand. Then coming close to me, he whispered in his garlicky breath, 'Is very very valuable. *Molto importante*.
I am custard 'ere.'

I nodded in agreement and tried not to giggle as drew slightly away from him and said,

'Thank you very much for opening your chapel.It must be a huge responsibility to be the custodian of such a magnificent work of art. I am so sorry if we interrupted your dinner.'

He looked mystified for a moment and then slapped his forehead again.

'My dinner, *si, si, la mia cena è attesa! Dio Mio,*' He slapped his forehead yet again as he added, '*Anche la mia donna. E una cuoca molto brava.Si, si, è una bravissima cuoca.* But the too many good cooks not like to wait and spoil the kitchen, no? *Scusate*, scusate* I must go back now. I 'ope another time, *si, si. Ci vediamo un'altra volta. Passa una bella serata!*'

8

By the time we reached the restaurant, the sun had finally given up and sunk behind the mountains. The sky still glowed a heavy red-gold, and the evening was warm, but I was beginning to be rather tired of the *bella serata* theme. Everything was somehow too *bella*. Jago was an immaculate companion, attentive and charming, if not showing any more of the passion that had lit his face when he looked at the Crivelli. The restaurant was very good, and as we were served a delicious assortment of tiny antipasti, I revived and rebuked myself for being so ungrateful. I shook my hair back over my shoulders and said,

'This is a great restaurant, Jago. Thank you so much for inviting me this evening. I am enjoying every moment.'

Jago looked down at the plate of *bruschetta* in front of him,

'On the contrary, Verity. I am so lucky to be sitting across the table from such a Titian beauty, your hair is outshining the sunset.'

It wasn't the first time I had heard the line. Titian beauty seemed to spring to the romantic lips of quite a few of the young men I had known at University, especially the art students. Somehow, coming from Jago, it held more substance.

'Are you an art historian?' I asked.

He frowned and gave a small grimace, 'For some reason that makes me sound very old and boring... but yes, I am writing a book on the Crivelli brothers.'

'Ah, I see, of course, that's why you are working here in Le Marche region.'

There was a brief hesitation and then, like earlier in the car, I noticed the small frown and wince of pain cross his face. There was something more, another reason why he was here in Italy. I was curious and said,

'But I suppose there are more Crivelli's in the National Gallery and around the world than near here. Why Macerata?

'What did you study when you were here as a student?' He answered quickly, but it wasn't an answer, it was an adroit change of subject. I could hardly pry any further.

'Italian language and culture.' I answered shortly and then added, 'Now, I'm trying to write a book.'

My words fell into the space between us, surprising me. I had no idea why I said it. Although the idea had been brewing in my head for some while, it was only yesterday that I had actually begun to write. I felt my cheeks burn with embarrassment, and I hurried on, 'Only a stupid idea, really. Nothing substantial yet.'

'Ah, that's the best time. The first excitement. Will you tell me about it? Is it fiction?'

'Oh, goodness, yes. Complete fantasy, I think.' I hesitated, then added, 'I want it to be a modern-day sort of Jane Austen novel. I hope that doesn't sound too conceited or silly.'

Jago sat forward and moved the candle from the centre of the table so that he could look straight at me as he spoke, 'Not silly at all. And I think one has to be conceited to write a book. Take me, for example.'

Suddenly he laughed and, possibly for the first time, I saw him relax. Now, he was very handsome indeed, and I instinctively reached my hand across the table to him. He looked at it for a moment and then held it and raised it to his lips and kissed it very gently. Then he laid my hand down onto the white tablecloth and patted it gently as he said,

'You are so young, so very young.'

I withdrew my hand as the waiter arrived to take away our plates. Jago spoke to the waiter in his impeccable Italian and ordered more water. With another swift change of subject, he said,

'There's an excellent natural source of spring water near here, further up into the mountains. Perhaps we could take a picnic there one Sunday?'

I nodded in agreement, and we continued to chat about mineral water, art, history, literature and a hundred other things. Jago fascinated me, and I was already looking forward to the idea of a picnic in the mountains... but, somehow it wasn't quite the *bella serata* I had imagined.

9

As soon as I entered my apartment, I heard my mobile buzzing and vibrating its way across the table. I snatched it up, too late as usual to catch the call. I bit my lip in impatience at myself. How could I forget to take my mobile with me on a first date with an unknown man? How my mother and Louisa, my ex-bridesmaid, would chide me. I looked at the small screen and saw that Hugh had called again. I sighed and decided the best course of action was no action.

I went over to the shuttered window and threw it open. It was only just past eleven o'clock, and I felt tired but restless. I poured myself a glass of water from the bottle in the fridge, then examined the label. Yes, it was from the same local source that Jago had talked about. I took the glass and went out onto the balcony. The moon was high above the rooftops, full and silvery. The scene was dripping with romance, but I had spent the evening discussing everything from sparkling water to old masterpieces. I sighed and moved my chair cautiously, not wanting any sound to reach down to Signora Brindisi. I had slipped past her door under cover of the noise of her television. I hadn't the energy to report back to her the events and non-events of my *bella serata*.
Then my phone rang again, its frantic little buzzing worming its way into my ear. I looked at the screen, thinking to see Hugh's name but saw it was Louisa. I quickly tapped the green spot and for once, caught the call.

'Louisa! I can't believe it. I was just thinking about you.'

'Really, Veri? Telepathy then? I've been meaning to call you for ages and ages. How are you doing? Are you having a great time? Is it hot over there? It's sheeting rain here. The racecourse and the Gallops are sodden. Are you surrounded by gorgeous Italian hunks as we speak? Have you heard from Hugh?'

This was a typical start to any call from Louisa. She always asked so many questions that it was impossible to know where to begin. I would generally pick the last question, but I did not want to talk about Hugh. Instead, I replied with a few questions of my own, and we settled down to a good long gossip. I told her something about Jago, something but not everything, as Louisa had a habit of running wild with her lurid imagination. I could hear music in the background as we spoke and I knew that she must be calling from our favourite club in Cambridge. For a moment, I felt a flicker of longing to be back there amongst our group of friends, laughing and dancing the night away.

'Are you calling from Diego's?' I asked.

'Yeah, I've just come outside for some air. The rain has stopped for once, and it's almost warm.'

Then I heard a voice call her name, a man's voice. Was it Hugh?

'You'd better get back to the party, Lou, let's speak soon.'

'No, no, he can wait for me a mo. You must tell me how your evening ended up. I mean, what time is it over there. Has your Jago guy gone home already?'

'Yes, yes,' I said hurriedly, 'Don't start dreaming up a grand Italian romance, Lou. It was just a lovely evening out to see some artwork and then dinner and... chatting. That's all.'

'Have I got this right? This Jago guy took you to see his artwork... in his Alfa drop-head and then you just talked? Come on, Veri, what are you not telling me?'

'Nothing, I promise, nothing more. We just talked of many things...'

Louise interrupted, and I could imagine her blonde curls bobbing around her face as she laughed and said in a silly voice,

'The time has come,' the Walrus said, 'To talk of many things: Of shoes and ships and sealing-wax, of cabbages and kings, and why the sea is boiling hot and whether pigs have wings. Ok, Veri, I give up now. Go back down your private rabbit hole in Wonderland. Maybe you'll meet the Mad Hatter tomorrow. Any girl who jilts Hugh Farley-Jones has to be completely insane anyway. Love you lots, though. Bye, *arrivederci, ciao ciao* and all that.'

Before I could respond, the line went dead, and I was left holding the silent mobile in my hand. I went back to sit on the balcony and to wonder if it had been Hugh, my Hughie, calling out to my best friend and ex-bridesmaid, Louisa?

'I wanna 'old your 'a-a-a-a-aand, I wanna 'old your 'and.'

I walked into my afternoon session and found, for the very first time, that my students were already in the room and talking, or rather shouting, excitedly. Flavio, in the midst of the tumult, was singing in a reasonably good Liverpool accent and an excellent baritone, louder than anyone, *'Oh please, say me, You lemme be your man...'*

I clapped my hands in an attempt to bring order to the chaos but as soon as they saw me, they surrounded my desk, holding out their phones, all playing music. I sat very still and smiled, then waited. Silence was something that I had found disturbed Italians. They were uneasy with it. At first, they competed with each other to get my attention, but when I remained quiet, they slowly, one by one, returned to their desks.

Flavio, the last to turn away, said very quietly, *'I gotta you babe.'* and then sat, not at his desk but on top of it. I raised my eyebrow at him and with a perfect shrug of his muscular shoulders and a return raised eyebrow, he slumped into his chair and stretched his long legs out in front of him.

'Good afternoon, everybody.' I said calmly but with determination

'Good afternoon, Professoressa.' Their sing-song response sounded like a class of primary school kids, and all the excitement ebbed from the room.

'Please turn to page nineteen.'

There was the usual low mutter of complaint and discussion between them as to the number in Italian. I was bored, and they were bored... and disappointed.

I spoke clearly and slowly. 'Today, we shall work on pages nineteen to twenty until four-thirty.' I paused, allowing them the necessary moments to calculate the time, then added, 'At four-thirty we shall translate the words from the songs.'

I wrapped the board rubber on my desk, sending a cloud of white chalk dust up into the air. The muttering ceased and, for once, the whole class looked at me, attentive and slightly alarmed. I spoke quickly before the silence broke,

'If I hear anyone speaking in Italian, then I shall not translate the words of your songs. Do you understand? No Italian from now on. This is an English class, and I am absolutely determined you will all pass your exams. Understood? Absolutely determined.'

To my surprise, I received a light patter of applause and Flavio, of course, it was Flavio, stood up and said,
'Brava, Professoressa, now we work like dogs, yes? A hard day's night, yes?'

I couldn't resist a smile, and the atmosphere in the room became almost happy. At last, I thought, as they scrabbled for the notes they had made of lyrics and passed them to Flavio. At last, I have their interest, even though it was slightly off-syllabus.

Flavio placed the pile of paper on my desk and gave a little bow before returning to his seat.

Then we began to work on the wretched textbook.

11

I smiled with satisfaction as I walked up the hill toward my apartment. The afternoon session with the group that I found I called to myself, Flavio's group, could hardly be persuaded to go home. Eventually, when the janitor had come into the room for the third time with his mop and bucket, I had called a halt. Was it my imagination or had Flavio rested his hand on the bare skin of my back as we had all moved through the door? Flavio, playing the part of the gentle shepherd herding me into his flock? No, I was quite sure he had very gently pressed his hand between my shoulder blades as he followed me through the classroom door.

I reached the entrance to the tall house where my apartment was on the top floor and went into the shadows of the cool hallway. I shivered, and for a moment every muscle in my body tightened but more to the memory than to the coolth. I stood for a moment to collect myself and to search for my key in my briefcase. As I found it and held it in my hand, I closed my eyes briefly and rested back against the stone wall, feeling the chill on my skin where the warmth of Flavio's hand still burned in my memory. Then I started and flashed my eyes open as a door opened, the back door to the garden and side road. For one insane moment, I thought it would be Flavio but, of course, it was my landlady, Signora Brindisi. She stood silhouetted in the bright light that now flooded into the hall. I blinked rapidly, adjusting my eyes and my equilibrium as she greeted me,

'*Signorina Gresham, ciao, ciao! Sta bene?*'
Now, she looked at me anxiously as I stood like an idiot, leaning against the wall and still blinking. I stood up straight and smiled,

'*Si, si, molto bene, grazie, et lei?*'
'I very well.'
'You speak English, Signora Brindisi?'
'Yes, little. I speak English from long years ago. *Una voltà,* once upon a time, I was the pair.'
'Pear?' I repeated in confusion.
'*Si, si*, I look after the children of very important family in London.'
'Oh, I see, you were an au pair? But you never told me.' I looked at her in shock and added, 'Why did you never tell me?'
'*Ah, beh!*' She looked slightly embarrassed as she continued, 'You speak the perfect Italian, my English very bad, very crusty. But, my daughter say me to speak English with you. Is good *opportunità*, you good teacher and my English come back.'
'Certainly, it's a good idea. I had no idea, of course, we can speak English together if you want. Your English is not so crusty, I think you mean rusty. Does your daughter know me?'

I spoke quickly, and Signorina Brindisi frowned as she made an effort to follow, but then she said,

'*Si, si,* my daughter Valentina, *la conosceva, si, si*. Valentina in your class.'

'Valentina?' I thought for a moment and then said, 'Of course, Tina, yes, I know her as Tina Tolentino.' As I spoke, I had a mental image of Tina's small dark face frowning at me from her seat next to Flavio.

'*Si, si*, Tolentino is my husband name.'

Signora Brindisi crossed herself quickly, sighing heavily as she remembered her late husband. She had shown me his photograph several times and talked of him sadly. He had died in a car accident ten years ago, and Signora Brindisi still wore black. I knew, too, that it was the custom for Italian women to keep their maiden names when they married, but the children more often took their father's surname. Tina Tolentino. I sighed and felt new sympathy for the young girl who always looked so ferocious and angry. Maybe, in her dark moods she was mourning the loss of her father. But Signora Brindisi was still talking and in hesitant English.

'Is not good girl, my Valentina, no, no, no!' She shook her head as though I had tried to disagree and carried on, 'Always, difficult, now, *ha venti-due anni ed è testarda. Come si dice,* how you say, *testarda*? *Mamma mia*, my English so rusty.'

I was silent for a moment as I thought how Tina looked more like fifteen than twenty-two years old and then said,

'*Testarda*? Well, in English I think we'd say 'headstrong'. The word *'testa'* means 'head' and '*forte*' is strong, yes, we'd say she is headstrong.'

I emphasized the 'h' sound and Signora Brindisi repeated the word carefully, imitating my pronunciation very well. I nodded in approval and thought how much better a student my landlady would be than any of my students. She had already changed 'crusty' to 'rusty', her ear having picked up my correction. Something of a pity, I thought to myself, but Signora Brindisi was continuing in full flow,

'Headstrong,' Signora Brindisi repeated the word again, and nodded with satisfaction, '*Si, si*, is very good word. I like very much. My Valentina is headstrong. *Mamma mia*, is very true. Last year she leave home and go with two friends to living in Camerino. Why? *Perque?*'

Signora Brindisi raised her hands and her eyes to the ceiling above where I now noticed more celestial cherubs cavorting dustily around the central light. Before I could make any answer, Signora Brindisi gave a resounding clap of her hands, wiping them against each other as though to dismiss the troublesome daughter from her mind and said in a cheery voice,

'*Allora,* now we have the *aperitivo, no*? We sit in my garden?'

'That would be lovely, *un gran piacere.*'

Signora Brindisi turned and went back toward the garden door but turned and said over her shoulder,

'Then, my English very rusty, I know, but I tell you all of your friend Mister Alfa Romeo, *si, si*, your new boyfriend, Professore Bradshaw. *Vieni, vieni*!'

I followed Signora Brindisi, very curious to find out what she knew of Jago in either Italian or crusty English.

12

Signora Brindisi's garden was small and chock-full of verdant plants. We sat at a round table under a pergola which struggled to hold in check the interweaving stems of a grapevine and the fronds of a wisteria. There was a small fountain wedged between two leafy lemon trees in large terracotta urns, and behind that, a gnarled olive tree fought for space. On the sunny side, possibly in pride of place, there were three shining silvery tubs, which I soon realised were washing machine drums, filled with rosemary and thyme. Between them, triangles of bamboo canes supported tomato plants, now laden with huge red fruits. Every centimetre was filled. On the table between our glasses, there was a beautiful Majolica pot of flourishing basil. I sipped the cool wine and thought briefly of my mother's garden. The neat rose beds and the herbaceous borders which constantly demanded her attention. My mother was a keen gardener and probably good at it, constantly pruning and weeding to control any excessive wild growth. Then, I remembered how she had planned the very spot for the marquee. I sighed and felt sad at the disappointment I had been to her. She loved Hugh, possibly more than I had. This thought made me smile, and at that moment, Signora Brindisi joined me at the table, holding a tomato that was so large it had developed creases in its shiny red skin. She placed it lovingly on the table next to the basil, and I knew she was planning a salad. She brushed her hand gently through the basil leaves and then, giving a sigh heavier than my own, she sat down.

'*Allora*,' She began, taking a long swig of her wine and smacking her lips with satisfaction, 'Is good to sit, no?'

'Oh, yes, and your garden is so lovely.'

Signora Brindisi laughed and said, 'Is what my Mrs Robertson say many times, everythings in the garden is lovely.'

I raised my glass to her and nodded, thinking how, apart from the odd sprinkling of the letter 's' in the wrong place, Signora Brindisi's English was losing the crust of rustiness very rapidly. I was enjoying the peaceful shade of the garden too much to correct her and replied,

'Yes, my mother says it too, when all is well. But...'

Signora Brindisi sat forward, and I found myself telling her everything about my sudden refusal to marry Hugh. She listened in silence until I reached the end of my sorry tale and then offered me a clean ironed handkerchief from her apron pocket as tears spouted from my eyes. I thanked her and wiped angrily at my eyes. I wasn't crying, but for some reason, my tear ducts had just overflowed. Signora Brindisi topped up my wine glass and pushed a small green bowl of olives toward me. Finally, as I sat refusing to sob and mopping my eyes, she said,

'I think you right. The marriage is very serious, no? You very young and plenty time. *Macché! Ciò che Dio fa è ben fatto.*'

At last, my tears had stopped, and I concentrated on translating in my head the complicated words of the idiom Signora Brindisi had used. I decided that a very liberal interpretation was that she thought I should try not to worry about the future. I exhaled which seemed very different to sighing, far more uplifting and I reached to the basil and imitated Signora Brindisi's action. The pungent bittersweet perfume of the leaves briefly filled the air, and now my all my sighing and exhaling changed to breathing in the beauty of the evening. I felt the tension ease from my shoulders, and I smiled at Signora Brindisi, who responded by pushing the bowl of olives nearer to me. I took one and nibbled it, enjoying the salty oily taste and added it to the delights of the evening. Then, Signora Brindisi took another long gulp of wine, smacked her lips in appreciation and returned to where our conversation had begun,

'*Allora,* your Professore, Mister Alfa Romeo. He work at the Università, *si si*, important man. *Allora*, my sister has a friend who has a sister who work there also... as cleaner.'

I was still working through the chain of contacts, from sister to another, when Signora Brindisi looked over her shoulder as though expecting to be overheard. She whispered conspiratorially,

'Is married, your Professore Inglese.'

13

After the initial shock, I realised that I had to be a fool not to have guessed that the charming Professore could be anything but married. But what Signora Brindisi carried on to say was verging on Jane Eyre territory. Not quite a mad wife locked in an attic but was it something like the modern-day version? Signora Brindisi's brown eyes rolled up to the heavens as she told me of the wicked wife who had deserted Jago three years ago.

'*Si, si*, now in New York. Poor Professore come live in Macerata for her and… whoosh, off she go!' Signora Brindisi threw her hands in the air, fluttering them like a bird on the wing and added darkly, '*Dio Mio*, is bad woman living now with… *come si dice*… opera singer.'

'An opera singer?' I stretched my eyes wide as the story unfolded and Signora Brindisi gave up on her English and continued in rapid Italian. Even if I hadn't understood her, I think anyone listening would have followed the story by her expressive hand gestures. I allowed her to carry on, or rather could not stop her as she elaborated on the wild affair that had taken place in Macerata, during a summer opera season. Through the chain of sisters and friends, she had learnt all the detail of the angry rows and Jago's desperate pleading with his wife.

'Is good man, your Professore.' Signora Brindisi was winding to the end of her tale now and she stood up, planting her hands on the table and looking down at me firmly, 'But he waits, he waits for his wife to return. Is sad man. *Si, si, molto desperato.*'

Then she grabbed the bowl of olives and turned away to go into the kitchen. As she reached the door, she turned back to look at me again and said,

'Now, I cook the *pasta, si*? Now we eat togetherness.'

And so we had eaten together and nothing more had been said of the Professore Bradshaw's sad affair or my escape from marriage to Hugh. We spoke of her daughter, Valentina, and Signora Brindisi's distress at her daughter leaving home. I tried to explain that it was only a rite of passage and that it did not mean that Tina loved her mother any the less. That, Tina only wanted independence and that Signora Brindisi should be proud. I spoke firmly enough, but I knew it was useless. My own mother had expected me to leave home and go to University but here, in the small city of Macerata, most families remained very close.

Then, after serving a delicious salad from the fresh-picked tomatoes in the garden, Signora Brindisi finally came to the point.

'Is a boy, I know it. Tina say she lives with two girlie friends but I know she in love.' She nodded grimly as though this was the worst possible scenario.

'But that's normal, isn't it?' I said, 'I mean, at Valentina's age…'

Before I could continue, Signora Brinidisi glowered at me from beneath her dark eyebrows and said,'

'*E normale, si*, when the boy love the girl but this is not.'

I wasn't now sure where the conversation was leading and thought I would continue in Italian, but Signora Brindisi continued, her voice low and angry,

'The boy not love my Valentina, is OK, no? He not must love her. But my Valentina, she headstrong, she not give up. Always she follows him like a sick dog.'

'Oh dear, that's horrid.' I said tamely, thinking about the sulky faced Valentina, the way she had of bearing a grudge against the world.

'Maybe she'll meet another boy soon.'

My voice trailed away and I heard my own words ring pathetically in the warm evening air. Did I sound like my mother? I thought of Hugh, then, and how I had hurt him. Maybe he would meet another woman soon? How many times had I ignored his phone messages? Unrequited love was a most unpleasant malady. Then Signora Brindisi's voice broke into my thoughts,

'My Tina is very stronghead, she not give up. She want Flavio and not other man in the world.'

14

Back in the peace of my own room, under my frolicking cherubs, I gave one of my longest sighs and then threw myself onto the bed. How could I have been so stupid? Of course, the sulky dark-haired girl that I now knew to be Valentina, Signora Brindisi's daughter… it was so obvious… she was hopelessly in love with Flavio. Perhaps they had been lovers and he had ended the affair? I looked up at my cherubs, hoping for some advice, but their plump faces smiled stupidly down at me, ignoring my question and then the next that had now slipped into my mind. Was Tina angry because Flavio was attracted to me? I placed my hand over my mouth as if to stop the obvious follow-up question even being considered. Was I attracted to Flavio? I closed my eyes to consider the matter and to prevent the cherubs from interfering with my answers. It didn't take more than a few seconds before my eyes flew open again, stretched wide as I knew there was no possible denial. Of course, I fancied Flavio, my heart was beating faster just at the thought. But would I be able to resist, that was the million euro question? There was certainly some Italian bureaucratic rule that teachers should not sleep with their students... apart from that...

I sat up and went over to the little kitchen sink to pour myself some water. The idea of sleeping with Flavio, or probably not sleeping but being in a bed with him and doing anything but sleeping, made my skin burn. I swallowed a tumbler of water and poured another and took it out onto the balcony. The night air was refreshing and I sat down to think things through more calmly. Perhaps I was going through some strange rebound thing after breaking up with Hughie? Only a short time ago I had been gazing across the candlelit table at the elegant Jago. The married Jago. What had that all been about? Was I going man crazy? Hughie, Jago, Flavio... just too many men in my life. Of course, I really should discount Hughie. I thought about him for a while, remembering his fond smiles and the comfortable ways we had developed between us. Shared holidays, days riding together, late-night clubbing in Cambridge, parties with our friends... all so easy. And how well we had fitted into each other's family lives. I shifted uncomfortably on the hard iron chair and idly picked some dead leaves from the geranium on the table in front of me. Would Hughie be out on the town right now... maybe in a group of our friends... maybe with Louisa? I poured the rest of the water in my glass onto the geranium and stood up feeling decidedly uneasy.

I leaned over the balcony and down to the narrow cobbled street below. It was late and even the Italians had finished eating and gone to bed. I knew I should try to sleep as I had my own day of study tomorrow, not teaching but learning. I rubbed my eyes at the thought of the proposed lecture on Ruskin's work and his book, The Stones of Venice. I went back into my bedroom and searched for my files and my copy of the book. Feeling a small spurt of energy, I went into the shower room and turned on the water. It was never hot but it was refreshing. I let the water run over my head and then slowly massaged shampoo through my hair. Some of the tension went from my neck and shoulders and I came to the decision that I should concentrate on my post-grad studies and teaching... and treating Flavio like all the other students in his group. I would be careful to keep my new friendship with Jago on the platonic base that he obviously wanted or at least seemed to want. As for Hughie, well, I should feel pleased if he went out with Louisa. Then, rebounding with some energy, I wrapped my towelling robe around me and took my files and book to bed. I settled comfortably to read, opening first the lovely leather-bound copy of The Stones of Venice and there on the first page was a message from Hugh.

'To my darling clever Verity on her graduation day, with all my love forever, Hughie.'

I closed the book quickly, blinking back the tears that had formed quickly behind my lids and threatened to trickle down my cheeks. Why did Hugh have to be so perfect? Always doing the right thing. Always patient, kind, generous and so, so wretchedly annoying. I turned on my side and curled up in a tight ball, thinking that now I would never be able to sleep. Then I must have fallen sound asleep.

15

The green slope of Newmarket heath stretched ahead of me and I sat forward in the saddle as my horse raced uphill. The wind was in my face and the first drops of rain began to fall. The clouds hung low over the copse of trees on the horizon and I just made out Hugh, on his dark bay horse, disappear between the trees. He was far ahead of me and I pressed my heels into the flanks of my horse, urging him to go faster. Now the rain was falling heavier, cold and sharp, hammering down and I had to blink to see ahead. Although my horse surged forward, I made no progress. The raindrops mixed with my tears now, hot tears of frustration and I tried to call out Hughie's name, but I could make no sound.

Then, in a second, I was sitting beside Jago in his car, a warm wind blew through my hair as we drove fast along a winding mountain road. Again, I tried to call out, but it was no good. Jago turned to me, but his handsome face was changed. He was angry in an excited way, his dark eyes stretched wide as he talked,
'The Crivelli paintings, the sheer mastery of the work, the colours so exquisite...'

But then, it wasn't Jago, it was Flavio looking at me, smiling as though he knew me well. Now, we weren't sitting in a car but side by side in my bed under the cherubs at Signora Brindisi's. I was naked, we were both naked and the room was very warm. Flavio reached out a hand and gently stroked my breasts, his fingers slowly circling one nipple and then the other. I arched my back in pleasure and he dropped his head to kiss my neck, then down, his tongue circling my erect nipples. His hands grasped my waist, pulling me toward him. I held him close, my hands running down his spine as I spread my legs wide.

Suddenly there was the sound of a gunshot… I awoke.

The room was lit by a flash of lightning and I saw the shutters banging in the wind and then there was a terrifying clap of thunder. I jumped quickly out of bed and over to the window. The wind and rain blew in at me, fronds of the wisteria thrashing around and soaking my thin silk nightdress, as I struggled to close the heavy shutters. A jagged bolt of lightning split the dark sky and lit the scene. For an instant, I saw the cobbles awash with a fast river of rainwater. Then, another booming clap of thunder quickly followed by more lightning. I thought, childishly, that there had been no time to count, which surely meant the storm was directly overhead. Finally, I managed to fasten the shutters closed. Now the room was dark and I stumbled over to the bed to turn on the bedside light. I clicked it back and forth but nothing happened. I sat on the bed in the dark, bewildered and shaken. The room was stuffy now that the window was closed and my rain-soaked skin dried quickly. I thought to take a shower but then decided that with a power cut it would be too difficult. Still, the thunder and lightning took rapid turns to terrify me. The claps of thunder so loud that the whole room seemed to shake and the lightning glanced through the louvres of the shutters, white and bright.

There was nothing to do but to wait and hope for the storm to pass over. I lay back on my pillows, trying to breathe slowly but with no idea of going back to sleep. I felt overwhelmed with a strange confusion. Had I been dreaming... more a nightmare than a dream? Yes, that was it. A clap of thunder that had woken me. I tried to catch the tendrils of my dream but failed to remember a thing. I lay back on the pillows and stared into the darkness until another flash of lightning showed the dancing cherubs above me on the ceiling, the gold of their wings glinting momentarily in the flash of white light.

Then I slipped into a dreamless sleep.

16

The next day was sparkling in perfection. A bright sun shone down from a clear azure sky, highlighting every roof tile and cobble. My ankle was completely recovered and I trotted happily downhill toward the University in my wedge-heeled sandals, the full skirt of my shoestring sundress flouncing from side to side. I felt good and, for some unwarranted reason, very pleased with myself. From the moment I had thrown open the shutters on the new morning, every shadow of the night's confusion and fear had dissipated like steam into the hot air. So, there had been a storm, the thunder had woken me from some strange nightmare... so what? Today it was simply good to be alive and not to be a teacher. Today, I was back to being a student at the University... all day.

As I ran up the steps to the University, I caught a glimpse of Jago ahead of me. I hovered for a moment before going through the swing doors. Did I want to catch up with him and wish him a merry *Buongiorno*? No, I decided quickly, and hovered for another moment giving him time to disappear through the long hall. Today, I wanted to study and not think about the three men in my life. I stood still for a moment inside the dark high-ceilinged hall, shocked by my own thought. Three men? What was I thinking? Number one, Hugh, of course... but hadn't I dramatically dismissed him from my life? Number two, Jago Bradshaw... surely a stupid romantic dream with his sophisticated elegance, his passion for Crivelli, Mozart, wining and dining, cruising around in his pale blue Alfa enjoying all the fine things in life... and married. I moved slowly forward as I considered the matter. Was it fair to lay any blame on Jago? True, he hadn't told me about his wife, but then he hadn't flirted with me either. Maybe he had regarded our outings to Monte San Martino and sunset dinners as nothing more than sharing time with another ex-patriot and colleague. I smiled to myself as I thought about that. Colleague? It was a ridiculous idea to think that from his elevated status at the University, he would even begin to regard me as a co-lecturer. I was here as a student and only teaching English part-time and at a lowly level. I carried on now, slowly moving up the big central staircase, still lost in my thoughts. But Jago had said my hair outshone the sunset... and that 'Titian beauty' line? Surely, at that moment, his dark grey eyes had glinted with the same passionate admiration that he had shown for his beloved Crivelli polyptych?

I reached the central landing and hesitated, wondering which way to turn as the staircase divided. I heard a burst of laughter coming from the landing above and looked up. There was Flavio, larger than life to remind he was number three. He was in the centre of his group of friends, arms flying as he held them all in his thrall. Tina was standing close beside him, looking up at him adoringly. I remembered Signora Brindisi's impatience with her daughter, *la testarda.* Somehow she didn't look too headstrong to me, more that she was swamped in hopeless love for Flavio. Then, Flavio, with his usual animal instinct, caught me looking at them and called out,

'*Professoressa! Buongiorno, Buongiorno! Come è sta?* Is beautiful day, no?'

He looked down over the wide bannister and smiled. I tried to ignore the fact that my core muscles contracted and my skin tingled as I waved back. I turned resolutely to my right, but Flavio moved swiftly along the landing and began to sing in his remarkably good imitation of Paul McCartney's Liverpudlian twang,

'Good day sunshine, good day sunshine, good day sunshine,

I need to laugh, and when the sun is out,

I've got something I can laugh about,

I feel good, in a special way, I'm in love and it's a sunny day...'

His friends began to clap along with the song, and Flavio suddenly vaulted over the bannister and dropped to his feet in front of me. I gasped and blinked in shock and took a step backwards, almost falling down the stairs. Flavio reached out and held me easily, both his hands around my waist, pulling me to safety.

Suddenly, my dream flashed back, running like a clip from a film. I had been naked in bed with Flavio, he was kissing my breasts. I drew my breath in sharply and the film vanished, but now, in reality, I was standing very close to Flavio and looking into his dark eyes. My nipples pressed against the thin cotton of my dress, and I longed to throw my arms around him, jump at him and circle him with my legs. My knees were turning to jelly now, and I drew in another longer breath and came to my senses.

'*Buongiorno,* Flavio. I'm very well, thank you. Yes, a beautiful morning.'

I sounded breathless in my own ears and Flavio nodded but said nothing. There was no need. He had read the lust in my eyes, in my whole body. He smiled and dropped his hands from around my waist. I forced myself to turn away from him but he lightly touched my shoulder and once again I felt a stab of desire as his hand rested on my bare skin.

'*A più tardi, Professoressa*, see you later?'

His last three words were more definite than a question. All I could do was to nod quickly and move on up the stairs. I was suddenly aware of his friends hanging over the bannister, watching. There, in the middle was Tina, her eyes dark with anger, met mine for an instant. Then, I turned the corner at the top of the staircase and went to my lecture.

The windows in the lecture room were cleverly high enough to make any chance of a distracting view impossible. I gazed instead at the fervent face of the lecturer. She was an intense woman, zealous in her ambition to explain the hidden depths of Dante's journey through Hell. I had to concentrate very hard to follow her gunshot speed Italian, but the room was too warm and I was finding it difficult. When she began to read in Dante's Tuscan dialect, I was temporarily lost until she glared at me suddenly and spoke in beautiful English.

'Despite its role in shaping the modern Italian language, today's Tuscan dialect retains some significant differences. The main feature separating standard Italian and Florentine is the phonetic characteristic called Gorgia Toscana, simply translated as the Tuscan Throat.'

Then she returned to reading from The Inferno.

I knew I was blushing, too aware that I had been caught day-dreaming. I sat forward in my seat and tried not to be distracted by the thought of a Tuscan throat. I blinked rapidly, trying to dismiss the sudden vision I had of Flavio... his face close to mine, his strong throat and prominent Adam's apple throbbing beneath his olive dark skin, his knowing smile as he held me close, stopping me from falling. I closed my eyes and allowed myself to enjoy the memory of his hands around my waist. Then, I flashed my eyes open as the lecturer was speaking in English again,

'O human race, born to fly upward, wherefore at a little wind dost thou so fall? Do you think this is a fair translation?'

To my horror, I realised she was speaking directly to me. I briefly turned around, desperately hoping that she was addressing someone behind me. Then she added in an icy voice,

'Verity, you speak very good Italian, I know, help us now with the idea that Dante is often poorly translated. How we say, *traduttori, traditori...* translators are traitors. Do you agree that a text can never be translated without some loss of nuance?'

I stood up, determined now to make a reasonable answer and not allow this daunting woman to embarrass me any further.

'Certainly, I am fascinated by the idea. Dante's decision to write in the Florentine vernacular, a sub-dialect of Tuscany, rather than in Latin was groundbreaking. He surely wanted his words to be understood by everyone at the time... the time being the early 1300's. Obviously, every effort should be made for a perfect translation.'

I spoke in English and then repeated myself in Italian and finally sat down. My heart was pounding but the lecturer was nodding at me in approval and clapping a flutter of applause. Fortunately, the bell then rang to end the session and I sighed with relief.

I quickly pushed my books and notes into my bag and made for the door. I needed some fresh air, but, for the second time that day, I felt smugly pleased with myself.

So, I had a silly, self-satisfied smile on my face when I bumped into Flavio. He was hiding around the first corner of the corridor that led from the lecture hall. I collided into him and made full-body contact and once again he placed his hands around my waist to steady me. Twice in one morning was too much for my courage to resist and I let myself relax into the hot comfort of his nearness. His dark eyes shone like jet from beneath his sooty eyelashes, his lips were curved in that smile that seemed to indicate he knew me well, knew exactly what I was thinking. Again my dream played across the retina of my memory and I briefly closed my eyes. We were naked in bed, my bed at Signora Brindisi's, Flavio was kissing my...

His voice broke into my reverie and I opened my eyes,

'Professoressa, you come?'

I stepped back a pace and looked at him in confusion. He continued, or maybe repeated what he had already said.

'Vuoi venire in spiaggia?'

'Do I want to come to the beach?' I translated like a robot, struggling to make sense of his question.

'Si, si, oggi... adesso.'

'Do I want to come to the beach today, now?'

I was still in translator robot mode and seemed unable to move on. This was harder than answering a question about Dante. I took another step back, hoping that putting some distance between us would help. Flavio was still smiling and for one second he glanced at my breasts and then back to meet my eyes again. We looked at each other for what felt like half an hour and then he spoke again,

'Con i miei amici.'

'With your friends? Er, yes... *si, forse...forse no?*' I shook my head, puzzled at my answer. Should I accept and go to the beach with Flavio... and his friends? Perhaps or perhaps not?

'*Ma si, professoressa, si...* is a beautiful day, no. I speak the English for you, all times.'

I couldn't resist a small smile at this and I knew that I had never intended to refuse the invitation. Why was I even hesitating? Somehow, Flavio guessed my lack of resistance and he clapped his hands together in triumph and began to sing in his McCartney voice,
'*Yes, yes!*
She's a big teaser
She took me half the way there
She's a big teaser
She took me half the way there, now
She was a day tripper
One way ticket, yeah
It took me so long to find out
And I found out
Ah, ah, ah, ah, ah, ah
Tried to please her...'
And so we made our way down the main staircase, causing some amusement and some looks of

disapproval. Just as we reached the main entrance I saw Jago. He was standing to the right of the door and watching the scene. Our eyes met for an instant and then he looked away as though embarrassed. I almost stopped, then, to go over to him but Flavio slipped his arm around my shoulders and swept me out into the sunshine.

18

And how hot the sun shone on that perfect day. The sand shimmered in the heat and the sea shone a translucent blue all the way to the horizon.

We had arrived at Porto San Giorgio early in the afternoon. Flavio had arranged everything in his easy way, giving me time to collect my beach bag from my flat and meet him again in the piazza.

Was I surprised to find him sitting in an open-top red Ferrari? Yes but then... no. It suited him so well that he could have been an advertisement for the car. He revved the engine as I arrived in the piazza and swung around to draw up beside me, then cut the engine and jumped over the driving door to greet me.

Surrounded as usual by his group of followers, there was then some noisy discussion about how many cars to take and who would travel with whom. Tina was there, looking even more murderous than usual and when Flavio ushered me politely into the passenger seat of the Ferrari, I should certainly have been dead on the spot if looks could really kill. To my surprise, Flavio had been very sweet to her and pulled his seat forward so that she could squeeze into the seat behind. I turned around to speak to her, but she pulled her knees up to her chest and sat sideways on the small bench seat behind me. I decided to give up on any sort of conversation and the noise of the high-powered engine soon made it impossible. I was prepared for Flavio to drive at speed but, in fact, he drove at a steady enough pace all the way down to the coast. The Beatles accompanied us and Flavio sang along in his rich voice, just occasionally glancing sideways at me and smiling, as though hoping for my approval of his English. I tried to stare straight ahead and not at his hands on the leather steering wheel... or his long muscled legs stretched out, his creased cotton shorts, his loose t-shirt flapping, his long dark hair streaming back in the wind, his tanned Roman nose... that throbbing Adam's apple... no, I hardly looked at him at all.

It was a glorious afternoon of fun, the sort of larking around that Italians do so well. There was a crazy game of football, some wild volleyball where they all cheated dreadfully... then ice-creams, sunbathing and swimming. The Adriatic was wonderfully warm and calm and by the end of the afternoon we were all exhausted and lolling around in the shallows. Flavio's friends ceased from calling me la Professoressa Inglese and I had become la Verità and finally, simply Veree. Even Tina had given up on being miserable and, apart from one rather sneaky shove when we were playing volleyball, she seemed to ignore me.

All afternoon I had been thinking of swimming out to the wave barrier that curved around the swimming area. Now, as everyone began to divide up, I decided it was the right time. I swam slowly, enjoying the movement of the small waves. Did I glance around, to see if Flavio was following me? Certainly not, I was clinging on to some remnant of dignity. I swam on and on, the rocks set around the concrete barrier were now clearly defined. I turned onto my back and floated, my arms stretched wide as I stared up at the impossibly blue and cloudless sky. There was a splash and Flavio surfaced right beside me, his handsome face streaming with water as he said,

'Ciao, Veree!'

Before I could answer, he duck-dived under the water and swam beneath me, emerging again on the other side, and immediately burst into song.
'So we sailed up to the sun
Til we found a sea of green
And we lived beneath the waves
In our yellow submarine
We all live in a yellow submarine
Yellow submarine, yellow submarine
We all live in a yellow submarine
Yellow submarine, yellow submarine...'

He dived under again and surfaced nearer to the rocks then raised his hand, beckoning me to follow him. I had already begun to swim and soon caught up with him. I laughed and shouted,

'First one to the rocks!' And I began to swim as fast as I could. Flavio soon understood and began a strong crawl through the water, hardly causing a splash in the blue sea. As he overtook me, I called out again,

'Oh no, I've lost my bracelet. *Ho perso il mio braccialetto*. Oh no!'

I held up my wrist and looked anxious. Flavio immediately dived deep into the water and began to search. I swam on as fast as I could to the rocks and pulled myself up onto the nearest. I sat for a moment, shaking out my hair and feeling the warmth of the sun on my skin. Soon, there was a shout of fury as Flavio realised he had been tricked. He swam easily toward me, laughing and shaking his head. I tried to look innocent as he pulled himself up onto the rock beside me.

'Sorry, Flavio, my mistake. I remember now...' I shook my arm in the air and added, 'No bracelet today.'

Then we were both laughing and he put his arms around me and kissed me. Oh, such a kiss. It melted me inside. He drew away for a moment,

'You, Professoressa, you very Veree *molto moltissimo ...che ragazzaccia! Si , si,* very Veree bad girl.' He kissed my forehead, '*Che ingannare!*' He kissed my right eye, '*Che birbante!*' My left eye, '*Arruffamatasse!*' Then the end of my nose, '*Truffatore! Stai barando... ma si bella*' My chin, 'Veree beautiful... *si bellissima...*'

Then our mouths met and he said no more for a while.

When our lips finally parted, we looked at each other for a moment and I don't know how long we would have gazed on if there hadn't been the sound of a car hooter. It was far enough away, but it continued, and we both looked toward land. I could just make out one of Flavio's friends waving and then saw the party was packing up towels and parasols to leave.

'Your friends are all leaving, Flavio, we should swim back. *Torniamo alla macchina*?'

Flavio jumped to his feet and climbed up to a higher rock and waved back. Then, with one of the hundred gestures that all Italians have up their sleeves, he indicated that he was staying and they should go without us. For a moment, I wondered how many girls Flavio had kissed on the same spot, quite forgetting that it had been my idea to swim out to the rocks.

Then Flavio was sitting beside me again, and we began to talk. What was it that my ex-bridesmaid, Louise had said... to talk of many things, of shoes and ships and sealing-wax, of cabbages and kings, and why the sea is boiling hot, and whether pigs have wings? So there we sat on the rock, close together, like the Walrus and the Carpenter. We spoke now in Italian, but I knew it would still be impossible to explain a quote from Alice in Wonderland. Would Flavio even have heard of the book? More likely, he would have been able to quote from Dante. He was talking now, quietly, about his family and his early boyhood and I listened carefully, but half my mind was absorbed in the vast difference between us... and yet, and yet, when we kissed again... it didn't seem to matter a jot.

19

We stayed on the rock for a long time, talking and laughing together. After our first passionate kisses, we had slipped into a calm mood. I leant against his shoulder as he talked and he held my hand, occasionally kissing it as I told him about my life in England. Finally, I told him about Hugh and how I had broken my engagement.

'So, is finish?' For some reason, Flavio spoke in English and his face was dark and troubled.

I replied in Italian, repeating several times how finished it was, but Flavio still looked doubtful. I began to regret telling him at all, but suddenly he smiled and shrugged and dived into the water. It was a perfect somersault dive and I waited until he surfaced before diving in myself. We swam, side by side, slowly back to the beach. The sun had dropped behind the hotels that lined the shore and the sand was pink in the dying light. As we paddled out of the sea and went toward our parasol the air was cool and I shivered.

'Is Adriatica! Always sun goes early.' He wrapped a large towel, still warm from the sun, around me and began to sing very quietly,
'Sunset doesn't last all evening
A mind can blow those clouds away
After all this my love is up
And must be leaving
It has not always been this grey
All things must pass

All things must pass away...'

His sweet voice was melancholic, the Liverpool twang suiting the mood and then he kissed me very gently on my forehead, and said,

'*Allora*, now we eat? Yes?

I nodded, suddenly feeling incredibly hungry and very much in need of some pasta and the comfort of Italian food.

Flavio was well known in the beach restaurant and I left him chatting at the bar to go and change. Looking in the pitted mirror in the changing rooms, I saw that my skin had turned a shade browner, but I was pleased to see not burnt. I quickly stripped off my bikini and stood for a moment, almost laughing at the neat white skin bikini that I was now wearing. I took a quick shower, the water only slightly warm and probably just heated from the sun shining on the pipes. Then I dabbed myself dry with a clean towel from my beach bag. What next, I thought, hoping that I had remembered to bring my Kaftan? Yes, it was folded neatly in the bottom of the bag, and I slipped into it quickly. I found my brush and pulled it through my wet hair as I looked in the mirror again. Not too bad, I thought, and then I twisted my wet hair up high and fastened it in a knot. Better, I nodded at myself and decided not to worry about make-up. I felt good, refreshed and even hungrier. I pushed everything into my bag and gave another glance in the mirror. I caught a glimpse of self-satisfaction on my face and frowned. Was it really the same day... was this the third time I had felt so pleased with myself, so smug... and all in the last twelve hours.

    I heard my mother's voice sound in my ears,
    'Pride comes before a fall, remember Verity.'

    I gave an Italianate exaggerated shrug of my shoulders, wrinkled my nose at my reflection and then turned away and went to find Flavio.

'*Mamma mia, mamma mia!*'

Signora Brindisi met me in the hall, her arms flapping wildly around her head, as I crept in at midnight like a naughty Cinderella. And, why was I trying to be quiet when the roar of Flavio's car could still be heard echoing around the cobbled courtyard and slowly disappearing into the night?

'You with Flavio Marcello?'

And why would I even think to deny it? The noise of the Ferrari was still reverberating into the distance and had definitely not turned into a pumpkin. I was quite sure that Signora Brindisi would have been hanging over her balcony watching the scene as I kissed Flavio '*buona notte*'. So, I nodded and said feebly,

'Yes, Flavio gave me a lift back from the beach.'

Now, Signora Brindisi nodded knowingly and tapped the side of her long nose then turned and opened the door to her kitchen.

'You take a glass of water?'

It wasn't really a question, rhetorical or otherwise and I went ahead of her, actually quite pleased to be invited. I was in that wide-awake state that often hit me when I knew I should be asleep. My mind was racing and my heart still beating fast from leaving Flavio. And I was confused.

Signora Brindisi ushered me to a comfortable chair near the open door to the garden. Then she fussed around cutting up limes and lemons, picking a sprig of mint and whacking a metal ice cube tray to make a simple glass of water into a cocktail. I sipped it gratefully and she stood watching me and waiting.

Of course, it wasn't long before I had given her a blow by blow account of my afternoon and evening. The first kiss out on the rocks, the romantic dinner in the beach restaurant, the drive home up to the hills with the breeze blowing through my hair... until finally, I reached the goodnight kiss and Flavio's sudden politeness and disappearance into the night. I had related my story in Italian, but now Signora Brindisi spoke in English,

'Flavio Marcello is good Catholic boy, strict family and very very rich.' Signora Brindisi rubbed her forefinger and thumb together in the international sign language for money. '*Si, si... ricchissimo!*' Then, raising her eyebrows, she added for good measure, '*Ricco puzzolente!*'

'Stinking rich?' I translated aloud and laughed as I thought that the red Ferrari should certainly have been a clue.

Now, nodding knowingly, she added, '*Elicotterri! Tanti elicotteri!*' And in case I hadn't understood, she circled her arm above her head and made a clop-clop-clop sound. Before I could take in the fact that Flavio's father was perhaps the king of the helicopter world. She threw her head back and added, '*Mamma mia, e veicoli blindati, si, si!*'

I was lost for a moment and it seemed that Signora Brindisi had run out hand gestures, but then, seeing my bewilderment, she acted out driving a car and then shooting a gun. I looked at her in shock and blurted out a rough interpretation.

'Vehicles armoured... I mean, armoured cars?'

'*Si, si*, many cars, biggy business, *un grosso affare!*'

'Really?' I answered briefly as my mind was whirring with this new information and leaping to the idea that Flavio's family business could be linked to the Mafiosi. But Signora Brindisi had moved on or rather back to where we had been in our gossip.

'But is powerful family, very Catholicky. Flavio, he talk about his Mamma?'

I looked at her in surprise at this sudden change in direction and replied,

'Well, yes, actually he talked a lot about his mother but...

Signora Brindisi interrupted me, 'Heh, my Tina she call him *un mammone ma...*'

Now I interrupted in my turn, 'A mamma's boy? Really, well, perhaps but...'

There was no stopping Signora Brindisi and she waved her hands at me,

'My Tina think this when he not interested in Tina, you know, he give her the cold elbow.'

'The cold shoulder?'

'*Si*, elbow and shoulder. She throw herself at him but no, Flavio is the good Catholic boy.'

'You mean they didn't, he didn't...'

'*Niente, niente*, nothing. I say you, Flavio is good boy and good Catholic. Now with you he stay good and serious.'

I considered her words then said,

'You mean, er, you mean, he...

'Yes, yes, he respect you.'

'Respects me?' I repeated her words like a robot, wondering whether I had strayed back from the 21st century and into a Jane Austen world or a chapter of my own ridiculous attempts to write.

'I think Flavio is serious for you.' Signora nodded wisely and tapped the side of her nose again.

I managed to stop myself from repeating her words and shook my head. Signora Brindisi struggled on, determined to use her English.

'Yes, he in love with you, he kissy you, no? *Allora... si, si*,...for sure. *Serioso*! He ask you to meet his family?'

I looked at Signora Brindisi, again in surprise at this next twist in the conversation. Just how had she guessed that?

'Er, yes, actually he asked me to go to his place for Sunday lunch.'

'No?' Signora Brindisi' hands flapped around her head again as though she was being attacked by a swarm of bees. *'Mamma mia, mamma mia!'* She followed this alarming display of something like fear with a rapid flow of Italian, the gist of which I understood to be a complicated mix of dismay and astonishment. Finally, running out of puff, she sat down in the chair opposite to mine and clasped her hands together.

'*Allora, non era una botta e via! Dio mio...* is serious.'

The more times she said the word 'serious' in English or Italian, the more I felt my own doubts. Was I being so English that I hadn't read the message Flavio was sending by being so restrained. Had I thought he would chase me past Signora Brindisi and up to my room, throw me on the bed for a night of passion? And wasn't that what I had expected and wanted? *Una botta e via?* My knowledge of Italian slang was quite up to translating that into a one-night stand or more literally a bang and go. But serious? Really serious and lunch with his family? Wasn't that fast work in another direction? Was I serious?

While the train of confused thoughts ran through my head, Signora Brindisi sat quietly watching me and I picked up my glass and finished the last drop of the icy water. She took it from me and then went to the sink and rinsed it under the tap. Speaking with her back to me she said,

'Tina never go to family house, *mai invitato*.'

I bit my lip wondering how I could answer that, but Signora Brindisi continued,

'My Tina, how you say, strong head always. After her father dead she go very wild. You know, she, how you say, *andare a letto con tutti amici*...?

I hardly wanted to translate that Tina had slept around with all her friends. As I hesitated, Signora

Brindisi carried on again, still not turning to look at me.

'Perhaps she want make the Flavio jealous, I not know but inamorataI very furious with her and off she go... all I know is that always she mad for Flavio. *Filament inamorata*!'

'Madly in love with Flavio? Oh dear.'

My response was totally inadequate and sounded ridiculously English in Signora Brindisi's small kitchen, but I could think of nothing more to add.

21

An hour or so later, I had showered and was lying in my bed, gazing up at my cherubs still cavorting around the ceiling. Was there now a spiteful glint in their blue eyes as they looked down at me lying beneath them, exhausted but unable to sleep. Even my little favourite with his bow and arrow had a slight air of dissatisfaction, as though he was tired of me. I yawned and rolled onto my stomach as I agreed. My life in Macerata had become annoyingly complicated. I rolled over again and turned on the bedside light. It was apparent I wouldn't be able to sleep, so I would read. I picked up my copy of The Stones of Venice and there on the inside cover was Hugh's hand-writing and message of eternal love. I snapped the book closed and put it aside and reached for the other book on my bedside table, Sense and Sensibility. I opened the page where I had left my bookmark, a thin strip of leather that Hugh had bought me at one of the Newmarket race days. I sighed, was there no escaping the men in my life? I tossed the bookmark aside and began to read,

"Eleanor went to her room where she was free to think and be wretched."

I smiled at how the words were so appropriate, so relevant, but then I couldn't read on. I felt too restless to concentrate, and I closed the book and placed it beside the other. I was now so wide awake that I decided to have another bash at writing. Maybe I would let my Genevieve character have another go at being in love, happy and carefree. I found my pen and notebook and sat at the table in the window. The air was cooler now, and the moon was high in the sky surrounded by clusters of bright stars. I sighed, long and loud at the thought of how very romantic it could, should, would be if Flavio was sitting beside me. I stood up and went out onto the balcony, still restless. The fronds of the wisteria moved gently in the night air and I brushed the tips of my fingers through the leaves. It was such a night for love. Then, angry with myself, I turned and went back inside and pulled the shutters half closed and fastened them. I took my notebook and pen over to the bed, lay down and began to write…

Genevieve sauntered…

Immediately I crossed out the name. How ridiculous a name and not at all suitable for my Victorian heroine. I scratched my pen through it, the black ink zig-zagging until it was completely obliterated. I began again…

Victoria…

no, too obvious… I scratched through the name and thought for a moment then I began again…

Beatrice sauntered down the garden path between the well-kept beds of flowers. The summer's day was cooling quickly as the sun slipped behind the small forest at the end of the garden. Her long skirt brushed the gravel as she walked and she was conscious of the pleasing sound of the rustling silk. Beatrice was well-accustomed to wearing silk and not at all aware of how it would be cleaned at the end of the day. Her life was and always had been extremely easy. Beatrice smiled as she snapped off of a tall purple lupin and waved it lazily through the air, swishing at the bees hovering above the flowers. She left the path and walked across the well-mown lawn toward a small wooden summerhouse. Beatrice had a rendezvous and she was late. Beatrice was intentionally late and she sauntered along slowly, enjoying the thought that her suitor waiting anxiously. Arthur was a very handsome man, and she had no real objection to idling away an hour with him. He would swear undying love, which was pleasant enough, and once again ask for her hand in marriage. He was as persistent as he was handsome and possibly more interested in her wealth than he should have been. Beatrice swirled the long lupin stem in the air like a sword and smiled at the idea of the duel ahead. She had often watched Frank, her brother, with his fencing master and loved the clash of the swords, the fleetness of foot. Yes, she would keep Arthur uncertain, parry and thrust. Beatrice made a few more swipes with the lupin and laughed aloud as she reached the door to the summerhouse.

'En garde, Arthur!' She called out as she entered. She stopped abruptly in the doorway. The summer house was empty. Beatrice drew in her breath sharply, so surprised that she twirled around the small room as though he could be hiding. Arthur was not to be found. She sat down on the long wicker sofa that stood in the centre of the shady room and threw down the lupin in annoyance. Arthur should have been obediently waiting, loyal as a lapdog. She stood up again and paced angrily around the summerhouse. She had no intention of waiting for Arthur. That wasn't at all how she played their romance. Then, to her further annoyance, the first large drops of rain began to fall. Beatrice sat down again and drummed her fingers on the arm of the sofa. The day was not going well and she was unaccustomed to any small difficulty. Now, she would have to wait until the shower passed over as she was not dressed for wet weather. In fact, Beatrice was seldom dressed for any unpleasant weather. She stood up again and peered out of the door. Heavy grey clouds hung low in the sky and large raindrops quickly splattered the front of her silk dress. She drew back inside rapidly, but just as she turned to go back to the sofa, there was the sound of rapid footsteps. A man ran in and collided with her, holding her close for a moment to steady her. Beatrice gasped in shock at the sudden hot proximity and the fresh grassy smell that surrounded her. Then he quickly stepped back a pace and gave a small formal bow,

'Signorina Hamley. Mi dispiace... le mie più sentite scuse. Please excuse me.'

Beatrice drew in her breath sharply and then replied, her voice high-pitched with excitement,

'You are the new Italian gardener?'

'Yes, Signorina, I arrived last week. Excuse me, please, I shall not disturb you.'

But Beatrice was very disturbed already. Her heart was pounding as it never had before. She spoke quickly, her voice regaining its usual soft timbre.

'No, please, there is no need for you to leave. It's raining very hard.'

'È vero... this is the English rain I have been told about.' He looked out into the rain and then bent to pick up the lupin stem. He inspected it carefully and then rubbed one of the dry furry buds between his fingers and collected the seeds. He took a brown paper bag from his pocket and sprinkled the seeds into it and folded it before pushing it into the pocket of his leather jerkin. Then he looked at her and smiled, 'But the garden is very thirsty. The soft summer rain is good, don't you agree?'

It was something Beatrice had never even slightly considered and she hesitated, trying to think of a sensible response. But her brain just wasn't working. Her body had taken over and she felt helplessly out of control for the first time in her life. He was so tall and yet muscled with heavy broad shoulders, his skin was tanned and his hair so dark and curly... and there was that aroma... fresh as new-mown grass and everything else of the wild outdoor world. She breathed in and took a step toward him as she said,

'My father wants an Italian garden, I understand. You are here to create it?'

'Yes, that is so.' He was looking straight into her eyes now and she held the gaze as she replied.

'Will it be easy? Will you enjoy it?'

'Why, yes, I am sure I shall.'

He gave a small smile and Beatrice glimpsed his perfect white teeth. Now she exhaled and felt her damp bodice tight against her skin. She was breathing fast now and she saw him glance down at her cleavage and was instantly glad she had worn her blue silk dress with the low neckline. But he was still talking,

'... measuring the extent of your land. I use my own body measurements... a pace, a step, my handspan...' Beatrice watched fascinated as he stretched his long-fingered hand out in front of her and longed to take hold of it, kiss it and draw it to her breast. But he dropped his hand and continued, his voice softer and lower,

'It is a slow process, intimate... unlocking the key to understand what the garden needs, slowly learning to know the garden as a man learns how to delight the body of a woman.'

It was too much for Beatrice, she moved toward him, slipping a shoulder out of her dress she took his hand and pressed it against her bare breast. Now, he gasped and suddenly lunged at her, pulling her other breast loose and dropping his head down. Beatrice threw her head back and let out a small primal cry of pleasure as his teeth nibbled gently at one nipple and then the other. Then, he gathered her in his arms and carried her to the wicker sofa. She reached for him and began to unbutton his breeches, aching for him deep inside her. The wicker sofa creaked as he laid over her, pulling up her skirts and pushing into her. She exploded immediately with a rippling orgasmic wave and he held still and hard for a moment, filling her completely. He began to move again, slowly and gently at first, the wicker creaked to a faster rhythm as she circled him with her legs, pulling him into her until everything in them both was spent and exhausted.

I put down my pen, shocked at my own words. I hadn't intended it to be so erotic. I closed my notebook quickly, not sure whether I would tear it up this time or not. Maybe I would wait until I read it in the cold light of day. I glanced at the window and saw the sky was slightly lighter. I checked the time on my phone and saw it was three-forty. I yawned and turned off the light, determined to sleep for a few hours and to be ready to teach in the morning. I closed my eyes but immediately heard a sound outside the window. I stared at the gap in the shutters and to my utter horror, I saw a hand moving to unfasten the lock. I wanted to scream but found I could make no noise. I pulled the covers up to my chin and froze. Now the hand was lifting the iron hook and pushing the shutters apart. A man's figure was silhouetted against the sky and I knew instantly it was Flavio.

'Veree, *permesso*? Is me, Flavio! *Disturbo*?'

'Flavio? Is it really you? Come in, *entra,* no, you don't disturb me, *vieni da me...* come.'

And so he did. And I soon found that Signor Brindisi was wrong in two ways. Flavio was not a good boy nor a good Catholic. And I was wrong, too, as he did disturb me in the most wonderful ways. He was so, so good. Even better than my Italian gardener.

22

That night had never been for sleeping. Lying exhausted after our love-making, we had talked. A continuation of all the cabbages and kings in the world, or at least in our two different worlds.

Finally, as the dawn light glanced in through the open shutters, I began to worry. Flavio, turned toward me, his hand resting on my hip, slowly caressing the angle of my bone. I looked at him, and suddenly, in the light of this new day, he became my student again. In a very few hours, I would be standing behind my desk facing him and his friends. Flavio sensed my abrupt change in mood and sat up, asking me what was wrong. When I explained that I would probably lose my job if anyone found out I was sleeping with him, he burst out laughing. I put my hand over his mouth to quieten him, aware that Signora Brindisi would soon be awake in her bedroom beneath us. Flavio held my wrist and kissed me, trying to stop laughing as he whispered,

'No problem.'

I sighed, these were Flavio's two favourite words in English. I continued in Italian, determined to make him realise the importance of what I was saying. When I had finished, he sat up in bed and shrugged, then declared that he would leave the University,

'No problem!'

'No, no, that's impossible, Flavio, you must pass your English exam so that you can take your law degree.'

Flavio looked amused and closed his eyes just long enough for me to admire his long sooty eyelashes. Then he explained in careful Italian that he had no interest in being a lawyer, that it was his mother's idea and that his father would be pleased to take him into the family business. Not only that, if he wanted a law degree it would be no problem. No problem as his father would simply buy him a degree. I was struck dumb at this but before I could recover to argue the point, he said,

'No problem! You be my private teacher, yes? Very private one to one lessons, *si, si*?'

Then he was kissing me and making love to me again. There was no resistance in me, and so I allowed the problem to be temporarily no problem at all. I lay back on the bed and pulled Flavio close to me, just for a moment I looked up at my cheeky cherub in the ceiling above and thought he winked. We made love quickly as though our bodies knew we soon had to be parted. Already we had learnt something of each other and the way we fitted. As we lay exhausted again, I heard the sounds of morning. Was that Signora Brindisi already in her kitchen making coffee?

'You must go, Flavio. You must go now.'

To my surprise, he leapt out of bed immediately and began to pull on his jeans.

'But, how will you go?'

Flavio looked at me in surprise, his dark eyebrows raised in perfect arches.

'No problem!' He pointed to the window and added, '*Grazie*, Veree, a hard day's night, no?'

He smiled at me wickedly and went to the open window and looked out. I jumped out of bed and joined him. He put his arm around me, and we stood for a moment looking at the pale dawn sky. Small birds were fluttering back and forth, gathering their breakfast. One landed on the wisteria branch and looked at us inquisitively.

'Oh no, Flavio, please don't climb down the wisteria. It's too dangerous.'

'No problem.' He kissed me on the top of my head and before I could hang on to him, he threw himself over the balcony and onto the twisted trunk of the wisteria. The little bird flew away in surprise, and I leaned over to watch Flavio climb down. My head swam at the thought of the hard cobbles far below, but Flavio looked up at me and smiled, hanging on with one hand and waving with the other. I managed a feeble wave in response and then to my surprise saw that he was climbing up again. I leant over the balcony, wondering if he had decided it was too dangerous, but when he reached me he stretched out and kissed my hand.

'Big problem to go, Verism.'

He looked at me for a moment then shook his head and began to descend again. I watched, my hands gripping the balcony rail in terror until Flavio jumped from the tree and landed like a cat on the cobbles. He looked up at me and blew me a kiss then ran off and out of sight.

I stood for a long while, trying to regain my equilibrium, waiting for my heart to stop pounding in my ears. I missed him already. Then I smiled at the idea that I was behaving like a modern-day Juliet.

'Wherefore are thou, Flavio?' I said quietly to nobody and then my smile changed to a frown as I went back into the bedroom, thinking how badly that had ended.

23

Lack of any sleep had not hit me when I left my room ready to face a day of teaching. Although I was nervous about the idea of meeting Flavio as my student, I was also looking forward to seeing him again. I was quietly humming 'It's a hard day's night ' when I reached the bottom of the stairs and found Signora Brindisi waiting for me.

'*Buongiorno, Signorina*, is a beautiful morning, no?'

I looked at her as she stood blocking the doorway, her arms akimbo.

'Good morning, Signora Brindisi, yes, a beautiful day.' I hesitated to say more and she frowned ferociously and then suddenly doubled over laughing,

'*Allora,* Flavio Marcello not so good boy?'

I felt the colour rush to my cheeks and stood awkwardly, wondering how to respond. Then, trying to control her outburst of laughter, Signora Brindisi said,

'Flavio only good boy with my Tina?'

Now I had no idea how to reply to that, so I struggled to change the conversation.

'Well, I must go to work now and...'

This only made Signora Brindisi laugh more and she spluttered,

'Difficult to work and no sleepy.' Then she pointed up to the chandelier hanging in the hallway and, unable to speak through her laughter, she waved her hand back and forth. I, too, looked up at the crystal chandelier, a cheap copy of Murano glass and realised it hung under the turn of the stairs... and my bedroom. Now, I was blushing to the roots of my hair and completely struck dumb. Fortunately, Signora Brindisi moved aside and with a slap on my bottom, pushed me out into the morning.

I hurried down the hill, still feeling Signora Brindisi's resounding smack and conscious of my rather tight-fitting t-shirt dress. Perhaps I should have worn something more teacherly for what could be an embarrassing day ahead. I began to hum again, still feeling the after-glow of the night and thinking that anything that occurred during the day at the University could hardly be more embarrassing than getting past Signora Brindisi.

But I was wrong. Outside my classroom, I found Jago waiting, a pile of books in his arms and an anxious look on his handsome face.

'Good morning, Verity. How are you?'

'Very well, thank you.' I answered cautiously, wondering if he had been sent to caution me about my behaviour with a student... and at the same time puzzling how anyone could yet know.

'How are you, Jago?'

'Very well, thank you.'

He pushed open the classroom door for me and followed me in. So far, so very civilised and English, I thought to myself, then turned around to find that Jago's eyes were riveted to my rear-view. Once again, I wondered just why I had chosen that particular tight-fitting dress. Then, Jago hastily looked up and said,

'I hoped to catch you for a word before your students arrive. I know you're usually an early bird. I mean... Goodness, I didn't mean to call you a bird.'

I laughed and relaxed a little, amused to see the impeccably sophisticated Jago for once ruffled. He continued,

'I'm afraid I'm rather nervous about what I want to say next...'

'Please don't be... ' I began, dreading that somehow he was about to tell me that I had been sacked for immoral behaviour with a student. Not only did I need the teaching post to keep my perilous financial status in place, but almost worse, a dismissal and a bad reference would jeopardise any further teaching work. I felt my stomach clenching at that thought and, rather to my surprise, I realised I enjoyed the work and that I was getting better at it. Jago was still clutching his pile of books and looking uncharacteristically ill at ease. I sat in the chair behind my desk, wondering how long I could call it 'my' desk and looked up at him,

'Do just tell me, Jago, what it is you are hesitating to say.'

'Well, I have two opera tickets for tonight's performance of 'La Bohème' and I wondered... I know it's short notice but...'

I almost laughed in relief and without thinking, I answered,

'Wonderful? I hadn't realised the opera season has begun. I'd simply love to come. Thank you.'

Jago's serious face lit up at my words and he struggled to hang on to his books as he tried to hold out his hand. Did he intend to take mine in a gentleman's agreement? I nodded and smiled and he began to back out of the door but, at the same time, my students began to arrive. There was a moment of collision, books fell and were collected again and with one last smile, Jago departed. I stood up to welcome my students, repressing any doubts that had begun to fly through my head. Would I be fired? Should I have accepted Jago's invitation? Then another group of noisy students entered, Flavio's friends. But Flavio was not in his usual central position amongst them. Flavio was not there at all... nor Tina.

I was beginning to wonder why I had, even for a moment, thought my teaching skills were improving. The class dragged on and on, the text book was not the best and the students were dreadfully bored. In the last quarter of an hour, I slapped my own book closed and suggested we translated some more song titles. This stirred a little enthusiasm but they all looked at each other as though unable to think without Flavio's input. I sighed, feeling every muscle in my body aching and my head beginning to throb. I mustered a sardonic smile, thinking how the class missed Flavio as much as I did, and raised the last of my energy and said,

'Think of an answer to this...'

I turned and wrote on the blackboard the words,

'With A Little Help From My Friends.'

There was silence for a moment as they slowly worked it out and then some laughter. I waited patiently, glad of the excuse to do nothing for a moment. Then, I felt my mobile phone vibrate in my pocket. I sat down quickly and pulled out my phone under cover of my desk. A text message from Flavio. I stabbed at my phone and quickly read the long Italian message. He was in Croatia with his father? The message continued, explaining that he wanted to tell his father about me and how he would be leaving his studies. That he had joined his father on a business trip as it was a good opportunity for a close conversation. There was more, but I skimmed through it quickly and the message ended with just a few words in English. She loves me, yeh, yeh, yeh.

I closed my phone and felt my heart beating rapidly as though I had been running. Did I love Flavio? I took a deep breath, scared at how fast Flavio was moving. But this was not the time to think about it or to reply. I pushed my phone into my bag and stood up. A tall girl shot up her hand, and I held out the chalk to her. She looked around shyly, giggled and then took the chalk and, copying from her mobile, she wrote,

'I Feel Fine.' Then she scuttled back to her desk, still giggling. Immediately a boy stood up and held out his hand for the chalk. I passed it to him and he wrote,

'Money, that's what I want.' He sat down again and everyone laughed and clapped.

Now there was fierce competition for the chalk and the lesson became lively and quite noisy. I knew they were using their phones to search and translate, but I made a fast academic decision and decided it was not any different from using a dictionary. It all carried on well and when the bell rang to end the morning, they left cheerfully, wishing me a cheerful variety of *buona serata, buona giornata and buon lavoro, ciao Prof...* the tall girl even managed to call out, 'Good day Sunshine!' without looking at her phone.

I thought this was possibly the first time any of them had spoken English aloud without repeating me and I gave a nod of thanks to the Beatles and their long-lasting fame. Then I turned to clean the blackboard until I reached the last line of chalky words,

'A Hard Day's Night.'

I paused, the board rubber in my hand and slowly erased the words.

Now exhaustion was beginning to overcome me and my eyes prickled with the dry heat of the room and possibly the start of tears. I rubbed the small of my back and then picked up my books and pushed them into my leather bag and made for the door.

Outside, leaning against the wall was Jago. He stood up straight as I approached and walked beside me,

'You look very tired, my dear. It's too hot for work, isn't it?'

I nodded, feeling too exhausted to reply. I had turned my phone off while I was teaching and now I longed to turn it on, hoping to find a message from Flavio. Jago continued,

'You don't have a class this afternoon, so why don't you go home to rest. Perhaps we could meet before the opera... about seven-thirty? Maybe an ice cream, I know you like ice-cream. During the opera season, I have a regular table booked in the little *gelateria* in the Piazza Nazario Sauro. I could pick you up and we could walk down through town together if...'

I interrupted him, suddenly wanting to stop him.

'Thanks, Jago, I know the bar. I'll be there at seven-thirty. I'm really looking forward to it. But you're right, it's so very hot and I must rest this afternoon. Until then...'

I waved my hand rather vaguely and Jago, the perfect gentleman, hurriedly nodded and with one last smile, turned and walked back along the corridor.

The University, one of the oldest in Italy, was a fine building and the corridor felt like one of the longest in Italy. I walked on, listening to Jago's leather-soled footsteps receding into the distance, and wondered if he was a perfect gentleman, just why he had checked to find out that I had no class that afternoon.

25

The sweet music soared up to the starry sky. The night was impossibly romantic. Jago had been waiting for me in the opera café, sitting at a table for two, set under the only palm tree that the place sported. It was so obviously the best table that as I approached, the other opera-goers stopped from sipping their cocktails to stare at me. I was pleased I had chosen to wear my demure but well-cut little black dress... the well-cut part being the way it dipped down at the back almost to the bottom of my spine. The front was cut high and square and just touched my shoulder bones. It was a great dress, and the moment I had seen it in a shop in Chelsea, I had known it was meant for me. Now, I realised it was also meant for this moment. I swung my way between the tables and looked straight ahead and at Jago. He rose as I approached and reached for my hand and kissed it. Maybe I imagined it, but there seemed to be a light murmur of surprise before the general chatter resumed. Yes, the evening had begun in a ridiculously romantic way.

Now, sitting beside Jago in probably two of the best seats in the arena, I sighed with pleasure. The sophistication of the occasion was not lost on me, the central position of the *poltrone*, the 'armchairs', and the expensively dressed and glamorous opera-goers on either side, clutching their sheets of libretto. I tried not to smile as I compared the excitement of my swimming race with Flavio to this elegant evening.

Comparisons were proverbially odious, and so I decided not to worry about it. Couldn't I enjoy both? Maybe Jago would never race out to the rocks with me, and I couldn't imagine Flavio listening to Puccini instead of his beloved Beatles... but... me? Couldn't I change like a chameleon? Without wanting to, I thought about Hughie. Had he shared all my interests? Certainly, we had both grown up to live and love the country life in Suffolk. Then, Hugh was obsessed with his horses and I had engrossed myself in my Italian studies... why hadn't it worked? I sighed and, once again, resolved not to worry but to turn my attention back to poor Mimi who was now singing her heart out centre stage.

I stole a sideways glance to Jago, his handsome profile gleamed in the moonlight and then I noticed that he had tears in his eyes. Instinctively, I reached out my hand and rested it over his to comfort him. He jumped in surprise and almost withdrew his hand from under mine, but then quickly took my hand and squeezed it lightly. He didn't turn to me, he still stared at the stage as though mesmerised. Now, I felt uncomfortable with my hand trapped in his, but it seemed impossible to withdraw it. I bit my lip and tried to remember how near the interval this particular aria would be. Adding to my discomfort, I felt my mobile phone tremble in the small side pocket of my dress. Maybe Flavio? I resolved to ignore it and returned my attention to Mimi who still sang on, her clear, pure voice filling the night air and sad enough to cause anyone to shed tears. I remembered, suddenly, that Signora Brindisi had told me that Jago's wife had left him for an opera singer. Perhaps the whole occasion was bringing back sad memories to Jago. Had Jago invited me for companionship and not intended it to be a romantic evening at all?

26

It was late when the opera finished and Jago and I walked slowly uphill through the town. We walked in companionable silence, not touching but comfortably in stride. The drama of the final act of the opera stayed with us. Maybe that was very English of us because the rest of Macerata was noisy with late-night excitement. The small city, usually so quiet by the midnight hour was buzzing. I smiled at the idea that it was not unlike Newmarket, usually a quiet enough market town, but transformed into hectic activity when there were race meetings or auctions at Tattersall's. Jago must have noticed my smile as he turned to me and broke the silence,

'I've booked a table at a small restaurant quite near your apartment. I was hoping you might feel hungry?'

I looked back at him in surprise,

'Goodness, I had no idea anywhere would still be open... but, yes, I'm starving.'

'Excellent! Right, come on then. It's just through here.'

He rested his hand very lightly on my back, steering me to the right and into a small cobbled alley. I was very conscious of his smooth hand on my skin and I walked quickly ahead and he let his hand fall away from me.

The restaurant was hardly more than a small terraced house. Jago knocked on the door and we waited. The only sign that it was a restaurant was a faded card in the window, the words '*Da Clara*' in wobbly handwriting. I strained my ears to hear any movement behind the door and Jago said,

'Clara will be there, don't worry. She's always busy in the kitchen. This place is unique. A colleague brought me here a year or so ago and it's the best food in town. Very exclusive... Clara practically has to invite you. Ah, here she is now.'

A key turned in the lock and the door was flung open by a small skinny woman who held out her arms to Jago and clasped him to her.

'Signor Iago, benvenuto!'

I stood back, waiting for the string of welcoming exuberant Italian words to end. Jago, then rested his hand on my back again and ushered me into the small entrance. I looked around and then shook hands with Clara who eyed me suspiciously and then hurried ahead of us down a small corridor. Jago added a little pressure to the area between my shoulder blades and then slid his hand very smoothly down a little, through the slit in my dress. I moved forward quickly and once again his hand fell away immediately.

The house was redolent of a wonderful mixture of cooking smells, too many to be identified and definitely reminding me that I was very hungry. Clara was still ahead of us and she went straight through a room that looked like a family dining room and outside to a small balcony. She pointed to a candlelit table set for two and Jago stood behind one of the chairs as I sat down. Clara nodded at us and then went back into the house.

'There aren't any other diners?' I asked, although it was a stupid question, hardly needing an answer.

Jago sat down opposite me and smiled, 'I know, it's a strange place but it's so very restful. Clara is an amazing cook, you'll see. And the view is so lovely.'

I turned to look across the balcony rail and saw the lights of the city spread out below us. It was similar to the view from my own balcony and I nodded in agreement. Then, thinking of the balcony and the climbing wisteria, inevitably, I thought of Flavio and quickly decided that it was a bad idea. I was here at Jago's invitation and I had been brought up to behave well.

'It's certainly different from any restaurant I've ever known. Do you think I could wash my hands?'

'Of course, the cloakroom is just to the left of the hall.'

Jago stood up as I left the table and I appreciated the gesture although somehow it made me feel the generation gap between us. Would Hugh or Flavio have stood up in the same way? My father maybe? It was an old-world custom but still carried charm. I went back through the dining room and met Clara, who smiled and directed me to a door in the hallway. The cloakroom, old-fashioned and spotlessly clean, was obviously used by the family as their coats hung on hooks and there was a rack of shoes. I quickly locked the door and pulled out my phone. Yes, another text from Flavio... and one from Louise and another from Hugh.

I sighed, thinking it was no wonder that I kept thinking about the men in my life. I opened the text from Hugh first, subconsciously saving Flavio's like a child saving the cherry on a cake. I read Hugh's quickly and immediately thought he must have been drunk when he wrote it. I checked the time and saw it was just after midnight in England when it was sent. After several mis-spelt lines of how much he missed me and still loved me, I was appalled to read that he had decided to come over to Italy to bring me home. I gasped with shock and switched to the next message from Louise. Her words were very unfriendly. I saw she had sent her message at almost the same time as Hugh. Had they been drinking together in a club? She told me in no uncertain terms that I was a miserable bitch to leave poor Hugh and in such a cruel way. That he was a wonderful guy and that I didn't deserve his undying love. I read to the end of her message, which continued in the same angry vein and not at all how she usually spoke to me. Something was going on in Newmarket that I didn't understand. Then, I switched at last to read Flavio's message. It was disappointingly brief and just said he had to stay on in Croatia for a few days and that he missed me. I turned off my phone and pushed it back into my bag, feeling flustered and confused. I looked in the oval mirror above the washbasin and saw my cheeks were flushed. I washed my hands in cold water and then patted my cheeks, trying to calm down. I frowned at myself as I pushed my hair back over my shoulders. Jago was waiting and this was not the time or place to sort out my life.

27

The dinner was extraordinary, easily the best food I had ever eaten in Italy or anywhere else in the world. Clara's husband a rotund silent man served each dish with reverence.

'Like Jack Sprat and his wife... and so between themselves , etc.' Jago smiled at me across the small table, and I couldn't help myself from thinking what a very attractive man he was, something of an early film star... Gregory Peck, maybe. I was just reflecting how he seemed from another generation when he startled me with his next sentence,

'I suppose you're too young to know it?'

'Sorry?' I mumbled, taking refuge in sipping the cold Verdicchio, 'How do you mean?'

'The old nursery rhyme, Jack Sprat. I don't suppose you know it. You're probably more the Peppa Pig generation.'

'Of course, I know the rhyme, my father quoted it every time I finished a meal. I was a poor eater and I think he used it as a reward. I certainly liked it. The idea of this happily married couple living in perfect culinary harmony.'

'I'm sure you were a clever little girl...well, you are now. Which rather brings me to a point I want to make quite clear? You are still a girl and I am probably twice your age so...'

'Oh, I'm sure you exaggerate, hardly twice my age and...'

'Yes, well, it's all very well but I feel like one of Nabokov's characters.'

'Are you comparing me to Lolita?' I said, laughing as I sat back in my chair. There was something so very appealing in Jago's honesty and I loved the very Englishness of his self-deprecation.

Jago laughed, too and shrugged,

'The problem is that I just love being with you. I don't seem to be able to help it. I've spent the whole day looking forward to seeing you tonight at the opera and now...' He stretched his hand across the table and I took it in mine. We looked into each other's eyes for a long moment and then, with a long sigh, he let my hand go again and picked up his glass. 'But it just won't do.' He put down his glass and said quietly, 'And, I am a married man.'

There was a silence between us and then I answered quickly,

'I know, Jago, I know you're married.'

He sipped his wine again and said,

'I suppose half Macerata knows the story of how my wife ran off with an opera singer. I didn't realise that you knew though.'

I couldn't think what to say next and he carried on, smiling ruefully,

'Ah, of course, Signora Brindisi, your landlady... she will have warned you by now.'

'I don't know about warning me but... but...'

'I know, there's little more to be said. Until I met you, I was desperate for my wife to return but now...'

We both left our sentences unfinished and there would have been an awkward silence if, just at that moment, Clara's husband hadn't arrived bearing a glass dish of tiramisu aloft. We both greeted it with relief and began to talk about the delights of food.

'Normally I don't take dessert,' Jago said, 'but Clara's Tiramisu is not to be missed. The sweet moment.' He looked at me again and his dark grey eyes were very sad as he added, 'You are the sweetest girl I've ever met but, in some ways, I wish you had never slipped over in the piazza... the day you broke your sandal strap... yes, I could almost wish that we had never met.'

I took a small spoonful of the creamy, coffee-flavoured dessert and thought about his words. Did I regret it? Did I regret coming to Macerata and falling into such a complicated scene? Before I could answer, Jago carried on,

'I used to take comfort in gazing at the Crivelli polyptych in the little chapel in Monte San Martino. The colours, the richness of the gold and the solemnity... well, everything about it gave me a sense of peace. I suppose that sounds ridiculous, it probably is downright ridiculous, of course. But now,' he gave another long sigh, 'Now, I seem to want to gaze at you.'

I decided I had to lighten the mood that seemed to have settled around us, so I said, somewhat heartlessly,

'My goodness, that does sound a bit creepy and Nabokovesque. I thought it was bad enough being called a Titian beauty but Crivelli? Isn't that a bit weird?'

I was relieved to find that Jago laughed at my words, really laughed and so the mood changed. We raved about the delicacy of the Tiramisu, the creamy ricotta, the subtle flavour of coffee and the lightness of the sponge. We moved on to talk about the opera and just when I was beginning to relax and think about going home, Jago said,

'You should be very careful about going around with Flavio Marcello.'

I almost dropped my spoon in shock and managed to feebly reply,

'Flavio? Do you know Flavio?'

Everyone in the city knows Flavio. His father is about as well known as the Pope around here... but not so popular. The Marcello family are very powerful. Maybe more like royalty than the Pope. Probably both are poor comparisons. The Marcello family rule this region. Maybe it's hard for you to understand exactly how life works in Italy. Anyway, you should know that Flavio's father gave a huge donation the University... at the same time as young Flavio became a student. Strange coincidence? Let's just say that Flavio Marcello won't have to work very hard to obtain a first class law degree. Just don't get involved. You should keep the young Flavio at arm's length and watch your back at the same time.' He smiled, trying to make light of his words,

'Goodness, I'm mixing my metaphors, aren't I?

Clara came out onto the balcony and I had no need to reply as we both broke off from our conversation and congratulated her on the meal.

It seemed as though Clara and her husband had the clever knack of interrupting conversations at the perfect moment. I don't know how I would have replied to Jago anyway. Arm's length was not quite the distance that I had held Flavio and, right now, my mobile was vibrating in my bag.

Of course, when I finally threw myself into bed... alone... I couldn't sleep. It was past two am and I knew I had to be up at seven but it was annoyingly apparent that my mind was racing too fast to even begin to feel drowsy. After half an hour or more of going back through the dinner conversation with Jago, I gave up and switched on the bedside light and reached for my notebook. I read back through my last attempt at writing and almost laughed aloud at Beatrice's seduction of the Italian gardener. Or was it by the Italian gardener? As I couldn't even decide who had seduced whom, it now seemed an implausible story to continue. I flicked forward to a clean page and began to write...

Beatrice ran...

I crossed out the first two words impatiently. It was no good calling my new heroine Beatrice. She was already too firmly a character in my mind even though I had no idea how she would continue to develop. No, I needed to begin all over again. I was searching my brain for a new name, a Victorian woman's name. I tried to recall Queen Victoria's daughters. Had there been a Louise? Then, of course, my speeding brain whirred off subject and I thought about my friend, my bridesmaid, Louisa. We had known each other for so long and shared so much, laughed so much... could she really be going around with my Hughie. But, then, he was no longer my Hughie, I had given up any right to call him that when

I had cancelled the wedding. Should I try to be pleased that the two people I knew best should now be together? I rolled over in bed and felt such a surge of anger that I knew I was a very long way to feeling any such thing. I curled up in a tight ball and hated myself. After a few minutes, I gave up on that and sat up, refusing to look up at the ceiling and the admonishing glare of the cherubs. So, I took up my notebook once more and began…

    Helena walked at a brisk pace along the clifftop path. There was a mild breeze blowing in from the sea and it lifted her soft curls and blew her skirts around her ankles. Her small King Charles spaniel ran ahead, rushing from side to side in a frantic search for non-existent rabbits. 'Here, Charlie, here! Come here!'

    Helena called but her words were blown away by the wind. She hurried forward, anxious now, as she saw a rider advancing and Charlie had a habit of trying to snap at horses.

    'Charlie come here at once!' She was shouting now, but again her voice seemed to disappear into the air. The galloping horse was drawing nearer and nearer, the sound of the hooves beating in the soft turf. The small dog stopped very still and then began to yap, not once but repeatedly. Helena had nearly reached him but the horse and rider were there first and Charlie sprang into action and jumped at the horse's hooves. Helena stood helpless aside as the horse reared up and she caught a glimpse of the rider's face, dark and angry above her. Then, she saw his hand holding a short whip, fly up into the air and down. Helena screamed and stepped forward, dangerously near the rearing horse. The man cursed and then settled the horse which was now snorting and pounding at the turf.

'Out the way, damn you, you stupid woman!'

The man's voice was loud and arrogant and Helena took a step back but glared at him furiously.

'How dare you, how dare you speak to me like that?'

His next words were quieter,

'Where's your dog?'

Helena turned around and searched the grassy clifftop and began to call again,

'Charlie, Charlie?' Her voice was now shrill with fear and the man slipped off his horse and stood, holding the snorting horse by the reins and said.

'Listen, keep very quiet.'

They stood close together in silence, straining to hear over the noise of the wind. At the same time, they both heard a small whimper from below them.

'Oh no, no.' Helena's voice lost its shrillness and it was almost a whisper as she continued, 'I think he's over the cliff edge.'

The man handed Helena the horse's reins and before she could think about it, he had thrown himself down onto the grass verge and edged forward until his head was hanging over the sheer drop. He turned awkwardly to Helena and said quietly,

'I can see him, he's not too far down. He's caught in a small bush.'

Helena made no reply at all. The horse was calmer now and tugged at the reins as he began to crop the grass. She was too terrified to speak. Her life was usually so peaceful and she was ill-equipped for any sort of emergency. An only child, she had grown up cherished and protected from any small discomfort. She was Helena Terrence of Terrence Hall and had never, ever met anything like the situation she now found herself in. She remained frozen with fear and speechless, breathless with shock as the man stood up and shrugged off his long riding coat. He threw it to the ground and without a word, lowered himself over the edge of the cliff. Finally, Helena found her voice and screamed out,

'No, no, don't...'

But the wind whipped the words away again and she was left standing alone on the clifftop, holding the reins loosely as the horse continued to graze at the short grass. Helena knelt down cautiously and inched her way toward the cliff top. The horse idly followed her and then stopped dead, too sensible to go any nearer to danger. Helena dropped the reins and threw herself flat on the grass and moved even nearer to the edge.

At last, she could see down the chalky rock face and to where the man was clinging perilously to a small shrub, the toes of his boots were digging and slithering, searching for a foothold. The sea, far below was pounding the shingle beach, large waves rolling in as the wind whipped the dark grey water into white froth. Helena was too terrified to call out, her head swimming as she looked down at the dreadful drop. Then, she saw Charlie, just below the man, whining piteously with his long silky curls snagged in a prickly bush. She couldn't even call out to him in case he moved or looked up at her. She felt an overwhelming sense of hopelessness, equally mixed with helplessness. Then, the man's foot slipped and he slithered further down the cliff. Helena closed her eyes unable to watch any longer until she heard his voice calling up to her.

'Are you completely useless, woman?'

She flashed her eyes open and saw that the man had reached the dog and was already tucking him into his waistcoat. He called out again,

'Don't just watch, woman, for God's sake throw my coat over the edge and hang onto the sleeve.'

Helena wormed her way back from the edge and reached out for the coat. Tears were pouring down her face as she grabbed it and, grasping the cuff of the coat, flung it over the edge. To her amazement, she heard the man laugh, not a small laugh but a roar of laughter that mixed with the wind. She looked over cautiously and saw he was looking up at her, his teeth very white in his tanned face as he continued to laugh.

'No need to knock us off the edge, woman, I thought you might lower it down a little more carefully. However, it will do. At least you held onto the sleeve.'

Helena twisted the rough tweed in her hand, making sure she had a good grip and waited. Charlie had stopped whimpering now and was licking the man's hand enthusiastically. The ledge of greyish earth and chalk where the bush grew was so narrow that Helena feared it would crumble away at any moment. Then she realised that the man was transferring the wriggling dog from inside his waistcoat and into the large slanted pocket of his coat. Charlie, with just his small snub nose showing, looked up at Helen with his glistening brown eyes.

'Charlie!' Helena managed to call his name but her throat was dry and a sob stopped her from saying anything more.

'Right, pull away now, heave-ho!' The man gave the pocket a small pat as though to send it on its way and Helena realised what she had to do. Slowly, remembering how wildly she had flung the coat over the edge, she dragged slowly at the coat, until with a last tug the dog was within her grasp. She rolled away from the edge, holding the dog in her arms, weeping with relief.

'Don't worry about me down here!'

The man's voice came up to her and she turned quickly and moved carefully back near the edge. Just as she reached the point where she feared going any further, the man's face appeared level with her own, still laughing he gave a kiss to the end of her nose and then, in the next second, he threw his leg onto the turf beside her and pulled himself to safety. They lay close together for a long moment, stretched out on the grass, panting until the man began to laugh again.

Helena sat up quickly, brushing the dirt and grass from her dress and touching the end of her nose where she could still feel the imprint of the man's lips. Before she could think of what to say, how to object at the rude kiss or to thank him for saving her dog, the man leapt up and held out his hand to her.

'Allow me, Mademoiselle.'

Helena ignored his outstretched hand and struggled to her feet, still holding Charlie close to her.

'Dear God, woman, you didn't even hold onto the horse.'

Helena looked around and saw the horse grazing peacefully some distance from them.

'Your horse is over there, sir, perfectly safe. Much as I am obliged to you for rescuing my dog, I have to object to you repeatedly calling me woman.'

To her annoyance the man laughed, another huge roar of laughter, and then slapped his thigh to show his thorough amusement.

'I see absolutely nothing amusing.' Helena said as haughtily as she could manage. Somewhere, deep inside her, she sensed a ripple of laughter that was bubbling to the surface of her anger.

'Quite right, quite right, Mademoiselle, nothing amusing at all about a grown man risking his life for a lapdog.'

As though knowing the man was talking about him, Charlie gave a sharp yap and, quite suddenly, Helena found she was laughing.

The man attempted to stop laughing and drew himself to attention and clicked his heels together, saying,

'A thousand apologies, Mademoiselle Helena Terrence of Terrence Hall, known only to me as the careless owner of the ridiculous dog,

Charlie. Permit me to introduce myself, I am Pierre Traverre, Comte de Traverre.' he then gave a deep flourishing bow and began to laugh again.

'Oh goodness, then we are expecting you at the Hall. I have heard my father speak of your arrival.'

She now stopped laughing and frowned.

'But on horseback? We expected you at least a week ago... surely in a carriage from Dover?'

'You're quite right, mademoiselle. My journey has been plagued with problems. My first boat from Antigua was captured by pirates, overcoming that little difficulty I found passage on a clipper... again, I apologise for my language earlier, I have been too long amongst common sailors. Finally, arriving in Dover, I purchased the fine somewhat nervy horse grazing over there, as the quickest way to get to Terrence Hall. Quickest and safest as by now I quite expected a coach to be stopped by highwaymen.' He gave another roar of laugher and bent double, slapping both hands on his knees and added,

'Then, as I finally drawn near to my destination, the daring and dastardly Charlie attacks me!'

As they talked and laughed, they had drawn nearer to the horse. Pierre clicked his tongue and spoke in a soft gentle voice,

'Ca va aller, ma belle... reste calme et venir à moi!'

Helena watched entranced as he reached out and gently took hold of the reins. Her French governess had taught her enough French for her to understand his words. Why was it she wished he was talking to her in this new gentle way. Her heart quickened and she held her breath for a moment, then suddenly she was encircled by his arms and lifted high in the air and placed in the saddle. She let out a small squawk of surprise but made no resistance when Pierre sprang onto the horse and sat behind her, holding her tight with one arm. No resistance at all.

29

I awoke to the alarm buzzing from my mobile and my notebook across my face. Could it possibly be morning? Seven o'clock? I pushed the book away and struggled to sit up and turn off the alarm. The book fell to the floor and then my mobile. I lay back flat and looked up at the ceiling and my cherubs.

'Don't say a word.' I said to my little favourite, thinking that talking to oneself was surely the first sign of madness. The alarm stopped but I knew it would soon be back, so I rose from the bed, found it and stabbed it off. There was silence then apart from the familiar sounds of Signor Brindisi in her garden, watering her tomato plants. How lovely to have such a quiet and orderly life, I thought, but at least didn't say it aloud. I sighed, thinking what a fine mess my own life was in. I picked up my notebook and it fell open at the last page of my writing. I read the last words and smiled. At least, there was only a suspicion of romance and no fervent love-making. Not yet, I thought although I could already imagine the next scene.

I contemplated taking the day off from teaching, from everything, and spending the day writing onwards. Why would this rather exciting Frenchman be visiting a Victorian gentleman? There were several interesting possibilities and I was tempted to pick up my pen. Then, my mobile buzzed with an incoming text message. I looked at it and almost turned it off. Could I take any more news? I reluctantly opened the message and saw it was from my student friend, Francesca. She was still in Paris but asked how I was getting on in Macerata. Well, that was difficult to answer, but I was pleased to hear from her. I replied quickly, dodging the question by asking another.

'When did she expect to be back in Macerata?'

I walked over to the window as I waited in case she would reply immediately. I opened the shutters and looked out across the rooftops, glad of the fresh morning air. My mobile remained quiet, so I left it on the table and took a long, cool shower. By the time I emerged, a towel around my head and feeling refreshed, I had decided that I would not skive off a day's teaching work. My students had only just begun to improve and I remembered that I had rather optimistically promised them they would all pass their exams.

As I made my way down the hill, an hour later, the sky was heavy with low clouds although the air was very warm for that time of the morning. As soon as I arrived at the entrance to the University, I saw Jago ahead of me. His height made him easily identifiable and he was taking the steps two at a time. I hung back, thinking I needed some time to think about our dinner conversation. Not just his declaration of love but also his words of warning about Flavio Marcello's family.

I walked slowly up the steps and Jago had disappeared before I reached the hall. I made my way quickly to my own classroom and took my place behind my desk. I still had ten minutes before the class started so I checked my mobile. I knew I should respond to Hugh and Louise, but I couldn't make up my mind what to say to either of them. There was still no reply from Francesca in Paris but there was another text from Flavio. It was written in emotional and passionate Italian words of love. I flicked quickly onto Google and found some Beatles lyrics and replied shortly and in English,

'But if you have to go away, if you have to go... now and then, I miss you.'

I was sure that Flavio would recognise the quote and the words were simple. I smiled with satisfaction, thinking that John Lennon summed up my feelings very well. Sometimes I needed Jane Austen's cleverness but this, yes this quote suited very well. I did miss Flavio... when I thought about him. I closed my eyes for a minute and succumbed to a moment of recall... his beautiful muscled body over mine, his sensitive hands running over my skin, how I had run my fingers through his dark curls, wrapped my legs around him and clung to him. Then, the first student flung open the door to the classroom and others followed. I flashed my eyes open, feeling the colour rush to my cheeks and tried to calm my breathing.

'Good morning, sunshine!'

The words were mumbled shyly by Tina. I stood up and smiled at her. Was this a breakthrough? It was certainly the first time she had spoken directly to me in Italian or English. I answered quickly but casually, hoping not to scare her away with anything too enthusiastic.

'Good morning, Tina.'

She nodded and then turned to give a dazzling smile to the boy coming through the door. To my surprise, he made his way quickly over to sit beside Tina with only a brief nod to me. In fact, he didn't sit beside her, he sat down and pulled Tina onto his knee and kissed her long and hard. There was a whoop of cheers and laughter from the rest of the class who were now all assembled in front of me. I wasn't sure if I should become teacherly and reprimand them, but I decided to pretend not to notice. I turned to the blackboard and wrote, 'The Weather', as a title and firmly underlined it. When I turned back to the class, Tina had resumed her own seat but, I noticed she held the hand of her new lover. She smiled directly at me now, another dazzling smile that lit her dark face and I realised how beautiful she was. I nodded, clapped my hands briefly and said,

'Today, we shall find vocabulary to describe the weather.'

There was a slight murmur of discontent amongst them, but I carried on resolutely,

'The English are obsessed with talking about the weather because it changes so much.'

I searched their faces for any sign of understanding but I knew I was losing them, I added quickly,

'In Italy you have beautiful weather.'

These simple words brought forth some interest and there was a spark of enthusiasm and several calls of *'La bella Italia'* and Tina's boyfriend spoke the loudest.

I looked at them sternly.

'Please speak English, only English in my classroom. Roberto?' I had suddenly remembered the name of Tina's ardent lover. 'Roberto?'

He stood up and said in a confident voice. 'Italy is beautiful and Tina is very beautiful.'

This produced a round of applause and some banging of their desk lids. I waited for the explosion of noise to subside and said,

'Very good, Roberto, very good. Now, who knows a song about the weather.'

There was silence for a moment and then muttering in Italian between them as they searched their mobiles. Tina shot her hand into the air first and I held out the chalk to her. She strode up to the front, swinging her hips extravagantly and almost snatched the chalk from me and wrote in large confident letters,

'Don't Let the Sun Go Down on Me.'

Then turned and handed me back the chalk. She muttered something in Italian which I thought was something like,

'Sei il benvenuto da lui.'

Had she said that I was welcome to him? I couldn't be sure and by the time I had taken in the idea of what she had meant, Tina was back in her seat again, hand in hand with Roberto. She raised her dark eyebrows at me and blinked her long dark eyelashes. Then, another student came up to my desk and I automatically handed over the chalk.

    The girl, one of Flavio's gang, wrote,
    'I wish it would rain down, down on me.'
    I nodded in approval and the lesson began in earnest.

The morning had dragged on as heavy as the sultry weather and I was just about to escape for lunch when the college secretary delivered a message. I was asked to call at the principal's office immediately. I nodded at the young man who delivered the message and told him that I would be there in five minutes. He nodded back without smiling and I felt my heart flutter. Had someone, possibly Tina, reported that I had been... the word 'fraternising' came ridiculously into my mind, fraternising with a student?

I made my way quickly along the corridor and went into the toilets. I needed a moment to think. I washed my hands in cold water and then splashed my face. As I patted it dry with a rough paper towel, I looked into the mirror that hung above the basin. I looked like a startled rabbit caught in the headlights. I looked guilty. I took a deep breath and pulled my hairbrush out of my bag. As I slowly brushed my hair smooth, I tried to calm down. I nodded at myself and decided that fraternising was probably the correct word but hardly described my passionate night with Flavio... my student. Fraternised had a friendly, brotherly ring to it. My school Latin came into my head for no good reason. *Frater*, brother, I muttered to myself and then thought how there was nothing at all brotherly about the way I had spent time with Flavio. I smothered a small, almost hysterical laugh and my reflection laughed back at me. No, that was definitely not the correct word but I couldn't think of another. More importantly, was I to be sacked? I knew the rules and it did seem very likely. My mind raced ahead as I thought how I would never get a reference to teach again... that I would probably lose my own place as a student here... that I would break my promise to my class as they might never now pass their exams... that I would have to return to England... and in disgrace. I watched my face in the mirror as the thoughts rushed through my head and felt tears of self-pity mixed with shame begin to prick behind my eyelids. Then, I shook my head impatiently and pulled my hair back, twisting it into tight knot and fastening it with a clip. I had to pull myself together. There was certainly no point in antagonising the Principal by dilly-dallying while he was waiting for me. No, I had to face the music. With a pathetic attempt at a brave smile, I shrugged at myself in the mirror and turned away.

I walked quickly along the corridor toward the main hall, trying to subdue the rising panic inside me and silently humming, '*Let's face the music and dance, there may be trouble ahead...*'

    I crossed the busy central hall, thinking how there was a song for every occasion. I passed the notice board where I had first seen the advertisement for my post as English teacher and saw it was now filled with new teaching posts for the autumn term. Such a short time ago that I had found my work and yet so much had happened. Too much. Then I reached the door to the Principal's study and tapped lightly on the door. My heart was beating loudly in my ears and I could only hope that my cheeks were not as flushed as they felt.

'*Entra. Avanti, avanti*!'

The words coming from inside were harsh and impatient. I pushed open the door and went in.

The Principal, a short, dark-haired man rose from his seat and held out his hand to shake mine.

'*Allora,* Signorina Gress-amm. Thank you for coming to see me so promptly.'

I shook his cool hand in mine, thinking that he had the only air-conditioned room I had found in the University and mumbled a small response. My voice was squeaky with fear, although this seemed like a friendly beginning. He continued,

'Please, sit down, Signorina.'

He spoke in perfect English, his voice silky smooth but I thought I could detect a coldness in his brown almost black eyes and he frowned as he continued,

'I wanted to see you about Flavio Marcello.'

His words made my heart pound in my ears again and I was glad I was sitting down. Before I could reply, he continued,

'Flavio is a student of particular interest to me, you understand?'

I nodded silently, unable to speak at all, remembering how Jago had hinted at the Marcello family influence and power and their funding of the University. I nodded, thinking that I was beginning to understand very well. Again, the principal continued, his voice oily now and slightly anxious as he held the fingertips of his hands together,

'*Allora*, I want to know exactly how well you know young Flavio.'

Finally, I managed a short sentence, attempting to keep my voice from squeaking.

'How well I know Flavio Marcello?'

My words were merely a repetition of his own and a poor response. Now, the Principal began to look impatient.

'*Si, si*, have you visited their home?'

I sat back in my chair, suddenly aware that the Principal had no idea of my exact relationship with Flavio. This interview was nothing to do with fraternising, this was something quite different.

'Flavio is a good student, enthusiastic and keen to learn. No, I have not visited his family home.'

I decided to keep my answers simple and truthful. Was there any need to do more? I had no idea what game the Principal was playing but I didn't want to be part of it.

'Then, why is it that he has decided to leave his studies? This would be very, very regrettable, you understand? A great loss to the University.'

I sat forward again, heart back to drumming and said, as innocently as I could,

'I sincerely hope he won't think of doing that.'

Well, that was the truth. Our conversation faltered on for a few more minutes and then I was ushered out of the door. I stood for a moment in the corridor outside and wondered about lying by omission. Is that what I had just done? I walked slowly back along the corridor toward the central hall as I continued to question myself. I had to admit that I hadn't answered the Principal with the full truth. I had thought myself to be an honest person until now. Then I began to think about the word itself, 'lying' and its two meanings. Then, straining to think like a teacher of the English language, my brain wandered on... lie, the noun, untruthfulness and lie, the verb, recline... loll...sprawl... stretch out? I exhaled, feeling a sense of hopelessness as I realised I had just about used the word in every way. Deep in muddled meditation, I had reached the hall, crowded now as students rushed off to lunch. Someone called my name and I turned around. Standing at the foot of the marble staircase, tall and blonde, was Hugh.

I knew it was ridiculous, but I pretended not to see Hugh. I turned my back and found myself staring at the notice board showing job opportunities. I read one or two, not taking in detail, but seeing teaching work offered in Sienna, then another in Bari and a small handwritten ad for an art tour-guide in Venice... then Hugh was standing beside me, and I simply had to turn around and face him.

'Hugh, whatever are you doing here?'

I didn't intend to sound so cross, but I saw a frown of disappointment on his brow. It was always so easy to know just what Hugh was thinking or feeling. When I had first met him, I had found this honest openness appealing but now... now, it was sadly annoying. I found I was clenching my fists and breathing hard, trying to keep my patience. I added,

'You shouldn't have come, Hugh, really not.'

I emphasised the last word, 'not' and he flinched and then said quietly,

'I miss you so much, Verity, so very much. I just had to see you.'

'I'm sorry, Hugh, really I am, but you have to believe it's over. I can't help how I feel, but I do truly regret realising that I couldn't marry you until we were so involved with the wedding... and everything...'

My voice trailed away miserably and, to my dismay, I realised that Hugh's light blue eyes were filling with tears.

'But Verity,' Hugh began struggling to speak, but I interrupted him quickly,

'Come on, Hughie, let's get out of here. We'll go to a café and have a talk.'

Hugh nodded and I walked quickly through the thronging students and outside. The day was still overcast and strangely sultry. I turned to Hugh and said,

'The weather's not usually like this, you've chosen the wrong day to arrive... it's so overcast and humid today.'

Hugh had followed close behind me and I was relieved to see he looked more composed as he glanced up at the pale grey sky.

'My usual luck.' He said rather miserably and then added, 'It's been splendid weather in Newmarket. Hot sunny days with spells of rain at night. Perfect.'

I sighed, knowing he was going to try to persuade me to return to England. I tried for a lighter note,

'Isn't it funny how English people always talk about the weather.'

'I suppose so, but isn't it more when they are just being polite or trying to avoid a difficult subject?'

I thought about that for a moment, admitting to myself that it was rather a shrewd interesting response. Not that I had ever thought him to be uninteresting, not exactly but... Before I could think any more on that subject we had arrived at my favourite café in the piazza.

The waiter, my favourite friendly waiter, came forward and directed us to table under a parasol.

'Buona sera, signorina, come stai?

I answered in Italian and we chatted for a moment about the unusual weather and then I ordered coffees and ice-creams.

'What were you saying, Verity?'

'Funnily enough, we were just talking about the weather. That proves it's not just the English. The weather is very strange today though.'

I looked up at the sky, cloudless and yet not the usual azure blue, then added, And I ordered you your favourite strawberry ice cream and a cappuccino.'

'That's it, you see, Verity, you know exactly what I like.'

I decided to change the subject, 'How's Louisa?'

'Oh... fine, she's fine.'

I looked hard at Hugh, waiting for any sign of guilt or embarrassment to show, but his face showed no change. I carried on,

'I thought perhaps you had been going out with her?'

Now, Hugh sat up straight and looked shocked,

'What the hell do you mean by that? Going out with Louisa? You mean, like... God, Verity, give me a break. I'm in love with you. I'm not interested in some ridiculous rebound affair. Louisa's just a friend and no more.'

'Hmm, well, I'm not sure she gets that. I think she may be in love with you.'

'Rubbish! Louisa just sometimes drinks too much and then she's in love with anyone around. You know Louisa.'

The coffee and ice-cream arrived at that moment, and I decided to change the subject again.

'I think this is the best ice cream in town, coffee, too. I went to the opera the other evening and there's another really great café down near the Sferisteria... but I still prefer this one.'

'Who did you go to the opera with?'

I hesitated, surprised by his instinctive response. I was tempted to say that I didn't need to go with anyone or that it was none of his business... but I shrugged and said,

'One of the lecturers from the Uni had a spare ticket, great seat actually... a *poltrona* ...which means armchair... right in the middle of the arena.'

'You're really into life here, aren't you?'

Hugh was looking woebegone again and hadn't even finished his ice cream. It had melted into a pink creamy pool and he stirred it slowly and said,

'I'm a fool coming out here, aren't I? You're not coming home.'

I nodded and felt very sad,

'I am truly sorry, Hugh. I know I've behaved horribly and you have every reason to hate me... not love me.'

'But I can't help loving you, Verity. I just can't help it. But I'll go away and leave you in peace. You should be happy here and I'm just making you miserable. I've found a small hotel near here, I'll go now.'

This was so sweet and kind that my heart was heavy with guilt.

'Do you want to see where I live? You can come up to my place for supper and meet my landlady, Signora Brindisi. Go on to your hotel later.'

I knew I shouldn't have suggested it as soon as I spoke, but it was too late to take it back. To my surprise, Hugh didn't jump at the offer but said slowly,

'Yes, maybe that would be good. I could tell your mother what your place is like then. She's so worried about you. Everyone is...'

I stood up resolutely,

'Well, there's no need for anyone to worry about me. I have a good job, some interesting Italian literature lectures and I've made some friends. I'm fine.'

Hugh stood up, looking very tall and English under the parasol and carefully placed a Euro note under the saucer. I noticed it was far too much for the ice-creams and coffees but said nothing. Hugh had a very relaxed attitude to money, never having been without it. Anyway, I thought, my friendly waiter would be delighted.

As I turned away from the table, I caught a glimpse of Jago just arriving at the other end of the terrace. He was with a woman, small and vibrant, dressed in an immaculate well-cut red dress. Jago held her chair as she sat down and didn't notice me at all. I moved away quickly and headed uphill with Hugh walking beside me.

We had walked almost in silence until we reached the small piazza that led to Signora Brindisi's house. Then, Hugh said hesitantly,

'I know you're only trying to be kind now, Verity. That's really not what I want. You don't have to ask me in.'

Until he said that I had been regretting my rash invitation, but now I felt even more guilty and said quickly,

'No, no, of course, you must come in and meet my landlady. She' so kind and I 'm sure Ma will be delighted to know you've checked out my living quarters.'

I had my key ready as we reached my front door but it opened and there was a beaming Signora Brindisi, pretending to be surprised. I knew quite well she must have been peeping through her louvred shutters and seen me arrive with Hugh. I was relieved and delighted to see her,

'*Buona sera*, Signora Brindisi, were you just going out?'

Signora Brindisi brushed away my question with a flourish of her arm and stood back to allow us to enter as she said,

'No, no, I let in the air only. Today is so so mugsy, no?'

I nodded and introduced Hugh, and she immediately clasped his hand and shook it, her eyes full of sympathy. I was beginning to regret now that I had told her everything about my cancelled wedding. That added to the regret that I had asked Hugh to come and see my flat made me nervous. Hugh, on the other hand, seemed entirely at ease and said,

'*Piacere*, Signora, sorry that is practically the only word I know in Italian. But you speak such good English. Not many foreigners would know the perfect English word to describe the weather today. It is, indeed, so mugsy.'

Signora Brindisi beamed and fluttered her eyelashes at Hugh whereas I could have kicked him. Mugsy?

Hugh continued smoothly,

'I am so pleased to meet you, Verity has told me how kind you have been to her.'

Now, Signora Brindisi gave me a quick glance and then slapped her hand on her heart,

'*Si, si*, I love Verity so well. She is good girl.'

I decided that the exchange of flattery had gone on quite long enough and so, to end it, I said abruptly,

'Signora Brindisi, I was going to make tea and show Hugh my rooms... won't you join us?'

Signora Brindisi looked from me to Hugh and then back to me, finally she nodded,

'*Si, si*, great pleasures, thank you.'

I wasn't sure if Hugh smothered a sigh of disappointment, obviously he had hoped for more time alone with me, but he stood back gallantly to let Signora Brindisi take the staircase ahead of him. I ran ahead, hoping I had left everything reasonably tidy. I hastily unlocked my door and went straight to open the shutters and windows. It was certainly mugsy today and my rooms had never seemed so stuffy. Signora Brindisi and Hugh followed me in, and I invited then to sit on the balcony while I made tea. They took chairs each side of my little table and while I waited for the pan of water to boil on the gas ring, electric kettles not being part of Signora Brindisi's cooking apparatus for her tenants, I was amused to eavesdrop on their conversation. They were quite happily talking about me and adding up my merits and faults.

'*Certo*, Verità, is content here in Macerata, she work hard at the Università.'

'Verity always works hard. She's very clever and she has high standards.'

'*Si, si*, I understand... you think she expect too much? *Troppo? Si aspetta troppo...* I think too. But she very clever girlie. '

'It's difficult to be good enough.' Hugh's voice was sad and Signora Brindisi said softly,

'Is better to be sure when you marry. Marriage is for long time. If is not right, is better to know.'

'I suppose so, but I miss her so much.'

'*Il tempo cura tutte le ferite, vero?* Time make better, no?'

'So they say but I don't know if I shall ever stop loving Verity and missing her.'

'*Ehi, ehi*, you not say that young man. You very beautiful boy, you find a lovely woman more right for you. *Pazienza!*'

The water bubbled in the pan and I poured it over the sprigs of mint that Signora Brindisi always gave me from her garden. I breathed in the delicate perfume that rose in the steam and then sighed. It wasn't just the weather that was heavy today. I laid the tray and carried it outside, prepared to try to lighten the mood.

The moment I set it down on the table, everything, absolutely everything shook. Signora Brindisi screamed and clasped her head in her hands and screamed one word,

'Terremoto!'

The cups and saucers rattled, the fronds of wisteria blew across the balcony in a sudden breeze and I realised the whole world was shaking. Hugh stood up and put his arms around Signora Brindisi who was crying hysterically. I clutched the balcony rail and looked down to the piazza below. Then, as though everything could not be more confusing, I saw Flavio standing below and shouting up at me,

'Entrare, vai dentro, Veri, go...go! *Giù dal balcone!'*

I stayed frozen for a moment and watched as Flavio ran into Signora Brindisi's house, then, finally galvanised into action I turned to Hugh and shouted,

'Earthquake, it's an earthquake, we must go inside! The balcony's not safe.'

Hugh nodded at me and somehow picked up Signora Brindisi and we rushed inside. Everything looked very normal in my room until the door flew open and Flavio burst in, the speed he was moving at carried him into the centre of the room. He came over to me and put his arms around me and pulled me to the door.

'Di sotto, di sotto... è più sicuro! Ma dobbiamo fare in fretta! Potrebbe esserci una scossa di assestamento.' Then he hurried me out through my door and down the stairs. I called back to Hugh,

'It's safer downstairs, there may be another quake.'

Signora Brindisi was whimpering now and Hugh managed to carry her down after us and into the small hallway. Flavio pulled open the cupboard door under the stairs and pushed me in amongst the brooms and mops. Hugh now understood and dumped Signora Brindisi inside onto a small chair and then looked at Flavio. Flavio nodded and they both crammed into the small space beside me. Signora Brindisi quietened a little and between sobs she continued to mutter,

'Terremoto, terremoto!'

I tried to pat her shoulder but there was hardly room to move. Flavio, standing very close to Hugh looked him straight in the eye and said in English,

'You are Huge.' It was more of a statement than a question.

33

We had stayed squashed into the cupboard for a good half hour, but the earth decided not to move again. Conversation was impossible, not to mention embarrassing. By the time my heart had stopped thumping and Signora Brindisi had stopped sobbing there seemed little I could say. It was hardly the time or place to formally introduce Flavio to Hugh or even to correct his name from Huge. Now, another regret flooded over me as I thought how, that beautiful day out on the rocks, I had told Flavio all about my dramatic escape from marriage. I could feel perspiration running down between my breasts in the stuffy air of the cupboard. My right side was pressed against Flavio, my left against Hugh and a stepladder pressing into my back. I was dreadfully relieved when Flavio opened the door and we all fell out into the hall. There was the sound of police sirens outside and Signora Brindisi suddenly cried,

'*Valentina, mia figlia... ehi, ehi!*' And she began to sob loudly again.

Flavio pulled out his mobile and quickly tapped a number. To my surprise, he had a signal and was soon speaking to Tina. He passed the phone to Signora Brindisi who cried and spoke all at the same time. Flavio, Hugh and I stood awkwardly around her until with one last heaving sob, she gave the phone back to Flavio and said,

'Tina Okasy, *si, si. Tutt'OK*! She is with boyfriend in Porto San Giorgio.' She glared at Flavio as if for some reason this was all his fault, possibly including the earthquake.

Flavio switched off his mobile without another word and looked down at his Gucci loafers. There was an awkward silence and I don't know how long we would all have stood there if the front door hadn't suddenly opened. Jago stood in the doorway,

'Verity, are you all right?'

I managed to nod dumbly and he came straight across the hall and put his arms around me,

'You must be very shocked.' I didn't move but couldn't help feeling safer in his arms. Then releasing me a little, he patted me on the head and turned to Signora Brindisi,

'*È voi, Signora Brindisi, state bene?*'

Signora Brindisi nodded as dumbly as I had and Jago continued,

'*È possibile fare il tè o il caffè?* Or maybe we all need something stronger?'

He smiled at Signora Brindisi, who hurried into her kitchen and then turned and invited us all to join her. Jago, one arm still around my shoulders, ushered me ahead of him. Flavio and Hugh followed close behind, ridiculously colliding in the small doorway, their broad shoulders hassling to be through first. I almost laughed at the sight but smothered the impulse, wondering if I was indeed suffering shock and on the verge of hysteria.

Signora Brindisi, now in the role of hostess, seemed more composed. She opened her fridge and took a long bottle out of the small freezer compartment. She took it over to the dresser and found five small tumblers and then exclaimed,

'*Mamma mia, la mia pepiera! Guarda!*' She picked up the long green pepperpot that had tumbled off the shelf and looked around. It seemed miraculous that it was the only sign of disturbance when the whole world had shifted on its axis. Then, she poured some bright yellow liquid into the glasses and brought one over to me.

'*Il mio limoncello*, is do you good, no?'

I looked at the liquid and felt suddenly nauseous. I took it from her and my hand was shaking so much that I quickly set the drink down on the table at my side. Jago immediately noticed and came over to me and took my hand in his, holding it firmly,

'*Che gelida manina! Se la lasci riscaldar.*' He rested his hand on my shoulder and smiled down at me and added, '... you need hot sweet tea, not this stuff.'

I was grateful for his kindness and appreciated his quote from La Bohème. It was so apt and a good reminder of the happy time we had shared at the opera. It was true, my tiny hand was frozen even though the room still seemed warm and airless. Then, I noticed Flavio and Hugh both staring at me and then watching Jago who had begun to heat some water.

Signora Brindisi hurried to help Jago make some tea and I watched feeling helpless and strangely exhausted. The scene was all too much for me. It was unreal and had something of a film scenario or a theatrical farce about it all. Then Flavio's mobile rang and he began to talk. Hugh came across to me and said,

'You should call your parents before the earthquake is announced on the news in England.'

I nodded, still feeling slightly removed from reality but managed to mutter,

'Would you be so kind as to call them for me? Tell them I'll speak to them later. Please?'

My last word came out with a slight tremor in my voice and Hugh nodded,

'Of course, it might be best, you're sounding a bit shaken and that would certainly worry them.'

Jago came over with a cup of tea and I tasted it carefully. My hand was still shaking and Jago put his hand over mine to help me. The tea was sickly sweet but I managed a few sips and felt a little better. I sipped a little more and set the cup down. Then Jago's mobile rang and he, too, began to talk into his phone. All three men were now occupied with news of the earthquake.

Signora Brindisi turned on her television and it crackled into life showing a young reporter standing in front of a ruined building. It was a live broadcast and the woman looked as shocked as I felt, her hair blowing loose in the breeze and dust. I shrugged my shoulders and sat up straight, determined to pull myself together. Hugh was speaking to my father, reassuring and calm, Flavio was alternatively listening in silence and then speaking rapidly, Jago was just listening to whoever had phoned him but his face was very serious. The three men were so different and it occurred to me that the only common denominator between them was myself. I exhaled and again felt exhaustion and a strong desire to be on my own. Then, Jago closed his mobile and said,

'I have to go.'

He sounded so deadly serious that I said,

'You can't go... it's surely too dangerous to go anywhere.'

Flavio closed his mobile and said in slow English,

'My mother send car now.'

I looked at him in surprise and said,

'But why? Why is she sending you a car?'

'Veree, you come with me. Is big car, Jeep. Is safe at home, *la nostra villa è antisismico*.'

'*Antisismico*?' I raised my eyebrows even higher and looked away from him and then to Hugh and translated like a robot,

'Flavio's home is earthquake proof.'

Before Hugh could reply, Jago spoke again and I saw his face was ashen grey,

'The priest in Monte San Martino has been harmed in a robbery. One panel of the Crivelli polyptych has been stolen.' He spoke quietly and added, 'I'm sorry to leave you, Verity, but I must go to him.'

I stood up, all my energy flooding back, 'But it can't be safe to go, Jago.'

Jago looked at me, his handsome face determined, 'I'm sure it will be fine, don't worry, Verity, don't worry.'

I shook my head, 'If you're going then I'm going with you.'

Hugh stood between me and Jago and said forcibly,

'What's all this about? Verity you can't go anywhere, I'm sure it's best to stay here. Signora Brindisi's house has survived the quake... yes, it must be best to stay put.' I shook my head and Hugh, knowing me so well, gave a resigned smile and added, 'But if you're determined to go then I coming too.'

Then, like some ridiculous chain reaction, Flavio said,

'If you go, Veree, and if Huge go, then I go... and in my car.'

I looked from Flavio to Hugh and then to Jago and said,

'Then we all go.'

There was the loud sound of a car hooter outside and Flavio said,

'Is my driver.'

We all looked at each other then and if it hadn't been so deadly serious it would have been seriously funny.

Signora Brindisi broke the silence and said,
'Me, I stays home.'

35

    Flavio was driving slowly through the outskirts of Macerata. The driver had been dropped off at his mother's house in Piediripa, and now, the atmosphere inside the large 4-wheeled drive vehicle was loaded with tension. Jago was sitting up-front with Flavio, sitting forward with his seatbelt stretched as though he couldn't wait to arrive. I was sitting in the back with Hugh and feeling very uncomfortable. Not that the interior of the vehicle wasn't extremely luxurious... it was the proximity of the two men who had both been my lovers. I noticed Flavio glancing into the driving mirror, trying to watch me. I closed my eyes as I thought about it. It just wasn't my style of life at all. My friend, Louisa, was the type to throw herself into short-lived love affairs... not me. I flashed my eyes open as the radio suddenly filled the car with the voice of a highly animated Italian reporting on the earthquake. I sat forward, listening carefully and when the reporter stopped for a minute, Hugh said,

    'What was that all about? What did he say?'

    'The guy is reporting live from near the epicentre. Somewhere between Perugia and Norcia, I think. Magnitude 6.6...'

    'Good God, from what I remember of my geography A-level that's high. What the Hell are we doing driving around? Is Flavio so stupid that he actually thinks his black-windowed Jeep can save us from another tremor?'

I saw Flavio's dark eyes flash in the reflection of the driving mirror and I wondered how much he had understood of Hugh's outburst. But then the word 'stupid' was '*stupido*' in Italian and attached to his name it wasn't too difficult to translate. But still, I reflected, the emergency did seem to have improved Flavio's English. I briefly wondered whether I should include shock tactics into my lessons but then sharply reminded myself to come back to reality. I dug my elbow sharply into Hugh's ribs and said,

'You didn't have to come and...'

Before I could say any more, the heavy car skittered like a toy across the road as, once again, the whole world shook. First, the car swung to the right, terrifyingly close to the rocky mountainside, then it veered to the left running beside the small barrier that was all that was between us and a vertiginous drop. I stifled a scream of pure fear as Flavio clutched the driving wheel and the car regained its place on the road.

'Is OK, is OK!' Flavio almost shouted and then slowed the car down. Jago turned around,

'None of you should have come with me. Now, I suppose, there is nothing to do but continue. There is unlikely to be another aftershock for a while.' He turned back and looked at Flavio who was slowly increasing the speed again, 'Well done, Flavio, you did very well.'

Then, we returned to silence as even the radio had given up. I gripped the headrest in front of me and then looked out of the window. Apart from some sheep who were running in an unusual way around their field at the bottom of the valley, the landscape was completely peaceful. Perhaps the birds, too, were flying in unnatural patterns, swooping and diving in what could have been agitation. I wasn't sure. Maybe it was my own fear and imagination?

We were taking a different route to the one I knew through Sarnano, the road Jago and I had driven on our evenings out. The sun was low in the sky and the air clear. There was no sign at all that the world had again shaken on its axis. So, we travelled on for another half hour or more until, to my relief, the road began to climb and I saw Monte San Martino high on its rock above us.

Hugh craned his neck to look up and said,

'Is that where we're heading?'

I nodded, feeling sorry for Hugh who was so accustomed to the gentle hills of Suffolk. But I made no reply and Jago said,

'Take the small road around the edge of the village, please, Flavio. We can go straight to the chapel, not through the piazza.'

Flavio nodded but also said nothing. I wondered if he knew the village at all and whether he had ever been to view the fabulous Crivelli polyptych. Somehow, it seemed unlikely. Then, I wondered how Hugh would react to the beauty of its rich colours and dark gold. He had never accompanied me to trips to the National Gallery or the Tate. I had never minded at all, it was just how our relationship had worked. I had never been closely interested in his stud, preferring to ride and enjoy the countryside but not the business of horse-breeding and racing. Maybe we had too little in common. I certainly enjoyed being with Jago, admiring the Crivelli, the architecture of the little chapel, the opera... so much culture-sharing had been exciting.

Before I could mull over any more problems in my relationships with the men in my life, we arrived outside the chapel. There were two cars parked in front of the small cottage that clung to the side of the chapel. Jago jumped out of the car before it had quite stopped and ran straight through the open door of the chapel. I followed and was in time to see his look of complete devastation as he saw the left-hand panel of the polyptych missing. I went to stand beside him as he stood, almost buckled over, his hands on his knees, gasping with shock. I rested my hand between his shoulders and felt him shaking. To Jago, the attack on the masterpiece was worse than any earthquake. Then, I heard movement behind me and turned to see Flavio and Hugh striding up the aisle, shoulder to shoulder. I felt a hysterical scream of laughter bubbling up inside me and the strains of the wedding march resounded in my head, dum dum di dum, dum dum di dum. I pulled myself together and stood up very straight as I said,

'Jago, the priest, we must go to see how he is. Didn't you say he had been attacked?'

Jago made no reply for a moment, and then, with a gasping sigh he stood up and said in a breathless voice unlike his own,

'Yes, quite right, Verity, quite right.'

He turned then as though to go back to the entrance, but he staggered. Hugh came forward quickly and held Jago by the arm, then supported him back down the aisle. I was beyond making any further wild, over-wrought comparisons to wedding scenes as Flavio put his arm around my waist and we followed Hugh and Jago.

There was no need to knock on the door of the cottage as it opened as we arrived. A small man carrying what was obviously a doctor's bag emerged and nodded at us, then made his way to one of the car's outside. Jago seemed to recover his equilibrium and quickly followed the doctor and spoke to him. I waited with Flavio and Hugh and then another man came out of the cottage. This time there was no evidence of his profession, but he was tall and moustachioed and carried an air of self-importance. To my surprise, he knew Flavio and greeted him like a long lost son. Hugh and I stood awkwardly waiting as they talked, first about the earthquake and then about the attack and the theft. Jago finished his conversation with the doctor and joined us.

'Fortunately, the priest is not concussed. He has a black eye but nothing too serious. But, the Crivelli panel...'

I interrupted, 'Thank goodness the priest is all right. That's the most important thing.' I looked at Jago severely and he had the grace to look ashamed as he said,

'Yes, yes, quite right, Verity, quite right.'

Now Hugh said,
'But art theft is serious, very serious. The altarpiece is remarkable... completely irreplaceable. We need to find out more. We must do something.'

I looked at Hugh with respect and some bewilderment. Perhaps I had misjudged his interest in art. But what, on this earth-quaking world, did he think we could do about it?

'So who was the man with the moustache that you were talking with, Flavio?'

Hugh gave Flavio an icy blue-eyed glare as he spoke.

We were all sitting in the restaurant awaiting our antipasti. I gazed out of the window at the sun setting behind the beautiful blue outline of the Sibillini mountains. It was so peaceful, so serene, that it was hard to believe the earthquake had ever happened. Inside the restaurant, nothing was peaceful or serene. We had been welcomed in by a trembling version of the jolly chef we had met when Jago and I had eaten here before. At first, I had thought it was a bizarre suggestion from Jago that we should all have dinner together. After a moment, as none of us seemed able to think of a better idea, we had agreed and piled back into Flavio's Jeep. Now, Flavio glowered at Hugh and replied,

'He is Sindaco in Monte San Martino.' Then he turned to me and added, '*Gli dica,* Veree, tell Huge, *Il Sindaco*...'

I interrupted Flavio and said angrily,

'You know very well his name is Hugh, not Huge.'

But Flavio just shrugged and flew into a torrent of rapid Italian. Jago, who was sitting with an untouched glass of water in his shaking hand, sat forward and listened attentively. When Flavio finally came to an abrupt halt, Hugh said,

'So, what was that all about?'

I sighed and sipped my glass of water, suddenly feeling very tired and I was glad when Jago spoke up,

'Apparently, il Sindaco, that's the town mayor, has explained that the insurance on the Polyptych has run out. Apparently, the security conditions were too expensive to install.'

'Good God!' Hugh interrupted Jago, 'Wasn't there any sort of alarm system?'

I caught Jago's eye for a moment and we exchanged sad smiles, both remembering the priest's careless way of describing how to switch the old alarm on and off. Had he even remembered it, anyway? But then Jago continued,

'Well, it was a rather basic alarm device but...'

Again, Hugh interrupted, 'But that's scandalous. A work of art like that not protected in any way? What did the police make of that?'

Jago shook his head, 'The police have not been informed.'

Now, Hugh sat back defeated in his chair, the perfect image of a shocked Englishman abroad, dismay at the foreignness of the situation showing in his every bone as he said,

'But, but why on earth, on this dreadful shaking earth, not? Why the hell not?'

All the time Jago and Hugh had been talking, Flavio had been on his mobile. He had moved away from the table to make the call, and I hadn't been able to eavesdrop. Now, as the antipasto arrived, he resumed his seat next to mine.

He rested his hand on my shoulder and, ignoring Hugh's angry glare, he said,

'Don't you know it's gonna be all right, all right, all right!'

I immediately recognised the Beatles quote but found it hard to believe that it fitted the situation. Hugh and Jago were both looking at Flavio, both angry now. Jago spoke first, his shock suddenly turning to real fury,

'What is that supposed to mean, Flavio? Just how can everything be all right? What are you talking about?'

Then, Hugh said,

'Exactly, no insurance, no police? Suddenly you speak English? So, tell me, just how is everything all right, you moron? '

I sighed again, weariness flooding over me as I thought how difficult it would be to explain Flavio's particular fluency in song lyrics and why did Hugh have a way of insulting Flavio in words that translated so easily? Stupid, moron... where to begin to sort them out before they came to blows. Even now, they were both standing up, leaning across the table, eyeball to eyeball. Then Jago said in a quiet teacherly voice,

'Sit down, both of you. Sit down at once. I believe Flavio has been speaking with his father.'

Flavio sat down obediently and Hugh followed suit. We all looked at Flavio as he smiled and nodded.

37

It was late when I finally arrived back at Signora Brindisi's house. Flavio had dropped Jago off in the main piazza near where he lived, so I only had to contend with Flavio and Hugh as they both tried to escort me to my front door. As they jostled shoulder to shoulder up the stairs and onto the small landing, my temper suddenly snapped and I turned to them,

'Will you both stop this right now. Go away, both of you. I just want to be alone.' I spat my words out in an angry whisper, hoping not to wake Signora Brindisi. 'For Goodness Sake, enough is enough. I'm exhausted and I'm going to bed... alone. Now go away, both of you.' Then I added for Flavio's benefit,

'*You say, yes, I say, no. You say, stop but I say, go, go, go! Vai a casa!*'

I glared at them both and they turned away and went back down the stairs, not pushing each other now but in an almost friendly way. I leaned over the banister, to watch them descend the spiral staircase, Hugh's blonde head bobbing down followed by Flavio's shining dark hair. Could they be more different? I exhaled slowly, confused at the thought that in some ways, I loved them both.

I turned and went into my room and closed the door behind me. I saw that my some of my books had slid off my desk and I bent down to collect them. There were no other signs of the earthquake, none at all. Once again, I found myself finding it hard to believe that it had ever happened. I threw off my clothes and took a long hot shower. Even the hot water system worked. Had Signora Brindisi turned the gas back on? Had it ever been turned off? My brain was racing with questions that I had no chance of answering. What did I know of earthquakes?

As I slowly dried myself, I had a moment of regret that I had insisted on being alone. Flavio would have known how life went on after the earth had moved. Hugh would have been kind and comforting, made me tea and tucked me up in bed. I went into the bedroom and lay down under the gaze of the dancing cherubs. My little favourite had his arrow ready to fly, his plump arm dimpled with the effort. I closed my eyes and immediately had a cinematic vision of Jago standing in the chapel, his face aghast. Was he now back in his home? With his wife? I flicked my eyes open at the thought and tried to decide how much I cared. Then, angry with myself, I jumped out of bed and went over to my desk. I picked up my notebook and read the last page. Then, I unscrewed my fountain pen. I gave a small sigh as I remembered that Hugh had given me the pen, a beautiful black Mont Blanc fountain pen, on my eighteenth birthday. I began to write...

Pierre urged the horse forward, trotting at first and then into a slow canter. The movement was...

I scratched my pen through the sentence, put the lid back on and threw my notebook back onto my desk. I was in no mood to write. I wasn't sure what mood I was in at all. I was exhausted and yet not sleepy. Empty and yet not at all hungry. I thought about calling home, but it was late and I had already told my mother that I was safe. I imagined my bedroom at home, quite large and comfortably furnished with the remnants of my childhood still around. Rosettes I had won at show-jumping, framed photos of my first pony, my books... ranging from Black Beauty to The Life of Leonardo da Vinci. Did I wish to be there now, surrounded by the solid, unshakeable facts of my life so far? I shook my head at the thought and went back to bed. I took some long slow breaths and decided that I was probably suffering shock. I nodded at my cherub and said aloud,

    'You're quite right, *il mio cherubino*, I need a cup of hot chocolate.'

    Feeling better from my self-diagnosis, I quickly warmed some milk and stirred it into the chocolate powder, reflecting that it was so much finer than any chocolate I had ever found in England. Was that it? Was everything finer, better in Italy? I took my mug back to bed and thought about that. Of course, it was a ridiculous idea. There were many things that were excellent about England. Now, my exhausted, agitated brain turned to the obvious question. Did I want to go back to Newmarket? I slowly sipped the comforting hot chocolate and spoke again to my cherub.

'No, no, no. I do not want to go back to my life in Newmarket.

He definitely winked at me.

I awoke to the sound of a tapping noise outside my window. I checked my mobile and found to my surprise that it was nearly nine am. I had slept a long and dreamless sleep, and I felt refreshed and ready for a new day. The noise continued outside the window. I jumped out of bed and pulled on my kimono. If that was Flavio playing the foolish Romeo outside, then he was in for trouble. I strode over to the window and threw open the shutters. The sun was bright and I blinked in surprise at seeing a ladder propped against my balcony. I peered out cautiously, drawing my kimono close around me as I caught sight of a builder's truck below and two men in blue dungarees inspecting the wall. I closed the shutters quickly and decided to take a quick shower and get dressed and ready for what the day had already chosen to throw at me. Was Signora Brindisi's house about to fall down?

Less than an hour later, I was taking coffee with a smiling Signora Brindisi and Tina. My anxious questions about the safety of the house had been quickly answered by Signora Brindisi. Apparently, Flavio had sent some of his father's builders to check out my balcony. I wasn't sure whether to be grateful or annoyed. Signora Brindisi, however, was delighted and so I decided not to worry or wonder about the power of Flavio's family. Surely, there was more important and urgent work in the area that day? I think Tina caught some of my confusion and said solemnly.

'Il potere della famiglia Marcello... è ovunque.'

She nodded, her young face serious as she looked at me. I met her gaze for a moment and then looked away.

There seemed to be no trace of jealousy as she spoke. Was she warning me when she said that Flavio's family power was everywhere? Was it similar to Jago telling me not to get involved with the Marcello family? I sipped my coffee thoughtfully, half-listening to Tina and her mother chatting happily together. They seemed to have completely forgotten their estrangement and Tina was telling her mother all about her new love. At least, here was one good result of the earthquake. I began to relax as I listened and the buzz of the caffeine renewed my energy. Then, my mobile bleeped a text message,

I peered at the screen, wondering which of the men in my life had decided to text me just when I was beginning to calm down. To my surprise and delight, I saw it was from Francesca, my good friend from my student days in Macerata. She wrote to say that she had flown back from Paris to be with her family after she had heard the news of the earthquake. She suggested we should meet up sometime later... maybe for a late lunch. I sent a quick text back to say how delighted I was and that I could meet her any time.

Almost immediately, my mobile pinged again, and I expected it to be her reply but saw that the new message was from Hugh. I almost laughed aloud as I read it. Hugh wrote to say that Flavio had invited him to visit their family stables to check out the horses after the earthquake. He would be back in Macerata later in the day. I pushed my phone back in my bag and felt the sense of contentment again as I listened to Signora Brindisi talking with her daughter. Did the strength of an earthquake have the power to bring people together? I was glad that Francesca was back in town and her family would be even more so. That Flavio and Hugh should decide to spend the day together was more surprising. They had been near to punching each other in the restaurant the night before. I knew that Hugh would be unable to resist inspecting any horses and that probably the Marcello family would have a fine stable of thoroughbreds. Hugh had something of the magic of a horse whisperer, and if the horses were at all disturbed then Hugh would be in his element calming them. I thought of Jago, then, and how he had shown a like talent, calming down Flavio and Hugh when they had stood eyeballing each other across the restaurant table. How mature Jago had seemed beside them, his quiet teacherly voice demanding respect . Only the damage to the Crivelli polyptych had managed to break his usual quiet control. My thoughts ran on and on until I realised that Signora Brindisi was asking me a question,

'*Allora, Verità*, what you do today?'

I came back to the moment with a jolt and had no idea how to answer her. Signora Brindisi was never the one to allow a long pause and she answered her own question, 'Tina say the Università close today, *allora*, so, you have the free time, no?'

I nodded and I was about to try a reply when my mobile rang.

'Scusi, Signora Brindisi, I'd better answer this. I have a friend back in town today.'

I scrabbled in my bag for my phone and tried to ignore Signora Brindisi heave a sigh as she waved her hands in the air and muttered darkly,

'*Mamma Mia, mamma mia...* another boyfriend? *Cosi tanti uomini nella sua vita!*'

Then she threw back her head and laughed and Tina clapped her hands and did the same.

I shook my head fiercely and looked at my phone screen, thinking it would be Francesca arranging where we could meet. I bit my lip as I saw that now Jago was calling me.

Signora Brindisi was entirely right. There were, indeed, too many men in my life.

Jago was in the café when I arrived, sitting on the edge of his seat and drumming his fingers on the table. There was none of his usual casual nonchalance, and I almost turned around and dodged our meeting. But I was too slow, and he had seen me and risen from his chair,

'Verity, good of you to come at such short notice. I simply had to see you.'

'Good morning, Jago... are you all right? You look so agitated and...'

'Yes, yes, you're quite right, I am in a bit of a state. You see I have been with my wife and...'

Jago had interrupted me so now I broke into his words,

'Well, that's good. Some sort of reconciliation then?'

I tried to keep my voice casual and friendly but not with much success.

'Absolutely not... that's why I had to see you. She actually wants a divorce.'

I sat down quickly in the chair that Jago was holding for me, feeling suddenly breathless. Before I could speak he continued,

'I never thought she would consider divorce. She's a devout Catholic, or rather, she was a devout Catholic. Now...' Jago stretched his long hands out to express his amazement, 'I can hardly believe it, but she has become a Buddhist.'

'A Buddhist?' I repeated the word stupidly, unable to think of anything to say.

'I know, unbelievable, isn't it? Apparently, she's in a group of new friends in New York and they're all Buddhists.'

'Oh, I see.' I said feebly, slightly worried that perhaps his wife had become involved in some sect. I knew of runaway teenagers who had been indoctrinated by weird religious cults, but it seemed unlikely with a middle-aged woman once married to the sophisticated Jago. I wondered why he was looking so elated about the whole matter.

'Her new man, the opera singer she ran off with, is taking up Buddhism, too.'

'I see.' I was cross with myself for repeating the same pathetic words but my brain was occupied with what Signora Brindisi had told me about Jago. Hadn't she said he had begged her to return and that he was desperately sad? I realised that Jago was talking,

'... and so we're going to get divorced. She wants to marry her opera singer and I...'

He broke off abruptly and reached across the table for my hand. 'And now I feel free to love you, Verity, with all my heart. I have loved you since the moment we met. That hot day when you slipped and broke your sandal. As a married man I had no right to even dream that you would think of me in the same way. But now...'

He was holding my hand tightly and I saw his beautiful grey eyes were dark with intense feeling as he added, 'I know there is a big age difference between us, of course, I know that, but we do share so much in common.'

He hesitated then and I realised he was waiting for me to say something... anything. I managed to nod and give a small smile and he added hastily,

'Of course, I know this is all very sudden and you must think about it. Quite right, quite right. I'll say no more now, but I'll wait. I'll wait for as long as you want.'

'Thank you, Jago. I am very flattered that you should think of me and it's true that we do have such a good time together but...'

He quickly kissed my hand and let it go, 'No buts, say no more now, I beg you. I can see you're confused with the whole idea. Just take whatever time you need to think about it.'

I nodded again, completely unable to think of the right or even the wrong thing to say. Suddenly Jago stood up, threw some money on the table and said,

'Right now, we have to go.'

'Go?' I looked up at him, this new energised Jago who hadn't even remembered to order me a coffee, and wondered what next. He shook his head in exasperation at himself and said,

'Dear God, I haven't even told you. The Crivelli panel has been returned to the chapel in Monte San Martino.'

'Returned?' I seemed to be unable to speak in anything but monosyllables.

'Yes, yes... Benito called me himself. He is quite recovered and called me after breakfast. When he awoke this morning, he found the panel wrapped in canvas and resting against the chapel door. Isn't it amazing? Flavio's family, the Marcello's must have been at work. We must go there straight away.'

I shook my head in disbelief but stayed seated as I said,

'I'm so glad Jago, it is amazing, but I'm meeting a friend for lunch so you'll have to go alone. Sorry.'

Fortunately, my dismissive parting shot to Jago was at least true. Or rather, it became true as Francesca and I agreed to meet for lunch in our next text message.

It was so good to see Francesca again. We had kept in touch ever since our time at Macerata University. I had only been there three months for my Erasmus term, but she had then stayed for a summer with me in Newmarket. We had the special sort of friendship that can be made at University, studying the same subject and finding, even though we were from different backgrounds, that we had so much in common.

We had reached dessert stage by the time we had caught up with the main features of our recent lives.

'Holy Moly, Verity, you have been rather busy here. I know Flavio Marcello… well, I don't actually know him but I've heard of him and his family. I'm not at all surprised that the Crivelli panel has been returned.'

'Do you think it really was Flavio's influence then?'

Francesca laughed, 'Why, of course. How else do you think it happened? Flavio told his Papa and that was that. Any criminal in the area would be terrified of disobeying Signor Marcello. I mean, maybe they were working for him but if not, if they were working on their own then…' She hesitated,

'I'm sure it's hard for a Newmarket girl to understand but…'

'Oh no, I get it. There's plenty of corruption in Newmarket, too. Do you think the Marcello family are actually Mafiosi?

Francesca looked over her shoulder as if worried that we might be overheard.

'Just leave it, Verity. It really is best to know nothing about it. As for Flavio, well, maybe you should try to cool it with him.'

Francesca slowly tapped her spoon into the caramelised surface of a small pot of pan cotta and sighed,

'Your life is so complicated, Verity, how do you expect me to advise you? I'm just a simple Italian girl with one ex-boyfriend in Paris.'

'Don't give me that, Frankie, you're not simple at all and you know it. And as you're my best friend, you just have to help me.'

'How about Louisa? She was your bridesmaid, wasn't she? Or would have been if you hadn't...' She looked across at me, her spoon held in suspension for a moment, *'Perché sei scappato?'*

Now it was my turn to sigh as I replied,

'I really don't know how to answer that? Why did I scarper? All I know is that, suddenly, I just knew I couldn't go through with it all. I just couldn't marry Hugh.'

'Hmm, well better to decide before the ceremony than regret it for the rest of your life. I expect you would have made Hugh perfectly miserable.'

'I seem to have done that anyway.' I muttered miserably.

'Yes, but at least he has the chance to get over you now. He'll find someone else... or someone will find him... *così attraente*. And as if it's not enough that he looks like a young Jude Law, he's so kind and gentle. He's a catch.'

'Yes, well, I think Louisa has her eye on him.'

'Oh, that would never do. I remember when I stayed with you in Newmarket, she was flirting around with a different guy every time I met her. No, no, no... Hugh deserves better than that.'

'I know, I know, Louisa is a bit of a tramp but she's so beautiful and such fun... maybe Hugh will fall into her arms on the rebound. Isn't that what's supposed to happen?'

'Hugh's far too grounded for that. It seems to me that you're more flapping around on the rebound.'

'Me? I'm not rebounding or flapping.' I looked at Francesca indignantly, then added quietly, 'Am I?'

'Well, you've been going on about the beautiful Flavio and the intelligent, elegant Jago all through our three-course lunch. I mean, it's not like you at all.'

'I know, that's the trouble. I've been with Hughie for so long that I don't know how to behave myself. I'm so out of my depth. Flavio sort of swept me off my feet. He's very sweet and not at all how he first appears. He's a good listener and so...'

'And so good-looking? Quite the Prince Charming?' Francesca laughed again and then suddenly added, 'Oh my god, Verity, you've already slept with him, haven't you?'

I nodded, feeling the colour rush to my cheeks. 'Only once.'

Then, the waiter appeared, as all good waiters do, with perfect timing, to ask if we wanted coffee. We looked up at him gratefully and both ordered an espresso.

I shrugged my shoulders and carried on,

'It was after our day on the beach.' I exhaled and gave in to the memory of that night and added, 'It was fantastic.'

'Oh my god, Verity, you haven't slept with Jago, too, have you?'

I sat up straight and frowned at Francesca, 'Certainly not, we're just good friends. He's such wonderful company, very relaxing and interesting and...'

'Phew, so you mean that Flavio isn't?'

I looked at Francesca in surprise, 'I don't know. I hadn't really thought about it.' I hesitated and then added, 'He's good company... you know, great fun and well, young, I suppose.'

'And this Jago's a lot older?'

'Hmm, well, he said he's probably twice my age, but I don't suppose he's much over forty.'

'Forty? More than forty?'

'I know, I know but he's very attractive and I sort of like the way he makes me feel special. But it's not just that, he's very clever and...'

'Oh my god, so you're teetering between having mad sex and fun with Flavio Romeo or going for an Oedipus complex with Jago. Or would it be an Electra complex? I don't know, but it's no wonder you're so confused. And that's without adding poor Hugh into the mix.' Francesca sat back in her chair and looked at me in some sort of dismay.

'I suppose so.' I answered miserably. 'And I haven't even told you that I'm trying to write a book.'

'Now, that's a sensible idea at last. I always thought you'd get round to writing.'

'Yes, I have always thought I would too... but whenever I begin a story it just turns to drivel. I can't sort of concentrate.'

'Well, that's hardly surprising, is it? Then the earthquake shook everything up. You know, we Italians understand the effects of a quake. It's new to you though. It's a very disturbing thing to feel the earth move beneath you. Don't underestimate the effect it will have on you for a while. Give yourself a break, Verity. Be kind to yourself.'

I felt a sudden relaxation within me at her gentle words. It was so good to have a friend to confide in and tell all my doubts. Then, the coffees arrived, and Francesca raised her small cup toward me and said,

'Do you know what, Verity, there are too many men in your life!'

She burst out laughing and I found myself smiling and nodding as I replied,

'I've just realised something, Frankie, and it's all due to talking with you. I've just had an epiphanic realisation.'

'Is epiphanic actually a word? I know I'm Italian and you're English and a would-be writer but honestly, epiphanic? Really?'

'Certainly, it's a word and it describes perfectly how I feel right now, this great Eureka moment of realisation.' I stirred the last of my espresso and looked into the dark grounds that stained the cup. 'You're so right, Frankie, there are too many men in my life and not one of them is the right one.'

'Er, is that a good thing or...'

'And what's more, I know exactly what I'm going to do.'

'You do?'

'Absolutely! I'm going to run away again, this time from all of them. I saw a job going in Venice and I'm determined to get it. Not only that, but I'm going to write a book.'

Aftershock

Two years later

It was Christmas Eve and Venice was even more beautiful than ever. I edged my way around the queue of people waiting to enter St Mark's Basilica for the midnight mass and hurried to meet Ben. It was our second Christmas together in Venice and I couldn't wait to be with him. The bright lights shone and reflected on every surface and, as I rounded the corner, I saw him waiting under the huge Christmas tree. My heart pulsed against my ribs as I ran to meet him.

'I thought you'd never get here, my love.' Ben held me close and I breathed in his familiar scent... spicy and warm.

'I'm so sorry I'm late. You must be frozen.'

'I'm OK but your little nose is a bit pink.' He kissed the tip of my nose. 'Come on, let's go to Alfredo's and eat.'

'Lovely, I'm starving. I thought they'd never go. Sorry.'

'Stop saying sorry. I should have been there to see your parents off. Were they on time for the plane?'

'Yes, we were at the airport early, but then the flight was delayed. I was beginning to worry that it might be cancelled.'

'Well, then they could have spent Christmas here with us. That would have been fine. I've arranged a motor launch to take us out to Murano tomorrow to see the glass Christmas tree and I've booked the table we had last year at the Osteria Murano. They could have joined us and I'm sure they'd have loved it all. Your parents are great company.'

    I looked up at Ben as we walked, arm in arm down a narrow cobbled alley toward our favourite trattoria. Did he really mean that it would have been fine to spend the few days of our Christmas holiday with my parents? Had he not noticed how my mother hated everything Italian and how my father went on and on about his horses? The only good thing about their stay in Venice had been that they actually approved of Ben. In fact, most of the time it had seemed that they approved of Ben far more than they did of me. I almost laughed aloud thinking about it and suddenly felt swamped with happiness.

    Before I could answer we had arrived at Alfredo's and Ben was holding open the door for me. We hurried into the welcome warmth and were immediately greeted by Alfredo's wife, Angelica. She kissed us both three times each and showed us to our usual table close to the pizza oven. I looked around at the chaotic Christmas decorations, the stacks of Panettoni behind a wonky tinsel Christmas tree and smiled. This was perfect, it was Christmas, I was with Ben and I had good news to tell him.

    'So, we'll eat the fish, yes?' Ben put down the menu without looking at it, 'Alfredo has been talking about his fish feast for days. It's not too late to eat well, is it?'

'That's one of the things I love about living in Italy, somehow it's never too late to do anything.'

I looked around the small candlelit restaurant and saw every table filled with people still eating.

'Of course, I want the fish. Isn't Christmas Eve, la Vigilia, supposed to be a light meatless meal in preparation for tomorrow? *Un giorno di magro*? Anyway, I told you I'm absolutely famished.'

'Famished and ravishing. You look so beautiful tonight, Verity. Your nose has returned to its normal pretty pale pink but your eyes are telling me you have something to tell me. Come on, tell me now. Before we start on the fish feast which is unlikely to be very light at all. Come on, I can tell you're dying to tell me something.'

I shrugged, amused at how well he knew me.

'Well, I have been waiting all day for some time alone with you. With my parents here there just wasn't the right moment.'

'You've heard back from that publisher, haven't you!'

I leaned across the table and gave Ben a light slap on his cheek and laughed,

'How did you guess? I hate you!'

Ben caught my wrist and then kissed the palm of my hand,

'I hate you, too, trying to keep secrets from me. Go on then, tell me what they said.'

I almost jumped up and down in my chair as I said,

'They want to publish it.'

Letter to Francesca

Dear Frankie,

I'm sorry it's so long since I wrote, especially as it was my idea to start writing proper letters to each other. I loved yours and read it three times over before I could take it all in. You and Hughie!!! I'm so so happy for you both. Why did I never think about it and do a Jane Austen type arrangement? Of course, you are both so utterly right for each other. Anyway, talking about Jane Austen I have some news about my book, the one I told you about that is a cheeky parody of Sense and Sensibility. I've just had a letter from a London publisher to say that they want it. They completely get the deliberately exaggerated imitation and, even more exciting, they're talking about TV adaptation. Have you swooned in a suitably Victorian heroine way yet? More anon on that subject because I have so much to tell you and my wrist is not used to this handwriting with ink thing that we agreed on.

So, next news item. You ask to know more about Ben. Well, apart from the fact that he is simply the most perfect man on the planet... and yes, you are quite right and allowed to say 'I told you so' several times because he is as beautiful as Flavio, as intelligent as Jago and as kind and gentle as Hughie... that's your Hugh! Ben's three years older than me (but much more grown-up), took almost the same degree in Italian culture and then came here to Venice to work as an art tour guide. Now he has his own business, meeting and greeting parties from the large cruise ships that dock out of the city at Fusina and Lombardia. He arranges the water shuttles into the city, art tours, hotels and restaurants... everything. That's how I met him, of course, when I took the tour guide job here, the one I told you that I was determined to nab. Maybe that was kind Fate intervening, il destino? It was definitely love at first sight. Amore a prima vista, un colpo di fumine... the whole whamming kaboosh! I mean, our eyes didn't meet across a crowded room or anything, but he interviewed me for about three minutes, told me I had the job and then asked me out to dinner. I knew I loved him immediately, no doubt at all. So, yes, you were quite right, there were too many men in my life in Macerata and all I needed was to find the one and only. I just wish I had been as clever and thought about you and Hugh getting together. Then I could wallow in smug self-satisfaction. Are you really getting married this summer? Well, of course you are and I shall be delighted to be your bridesmaid. I'll try not to behave like Louisa although my Ma tells me that she has settled down a bit and gone to work in California. Look out Californian men, I say.

    Next item. You ask about Jago. I had a letter from him about a month ago from Perugia where he is now living and working. He seemed so happy and wrote of hardly anything other than the restoration work on the Crivelli polyptych. He is documenting and recording every detail and he is planning a new book on the subject. He gave several passing mentions to a certain talented Professoressa Luisa Lombardino who works 'closely alongside'... his words! I do just wonder if it's his way of telling me that he has found a soul mate. I hope so.

Next item, well, more of a reply to your news about Flavio. I was hardly surprised that he dropped out of uni and his law degree. I couldn't really see him as a lawyer. I was surprised to hear that he's gone off to California though. Maybe Fate, il Destino will play another hand and get him to meet Louisa? Now that would be quite another story.

Oh yes, and thank you for telling me about Tina's engagement and how they have settled into my old top floor flat. Signora Brindisi will be so pleased and I think I know the boy you mean. I'm sure it's Roberto, he was in my class. Goodness, that's so strange to think I actually had a class of students. At least they all scraped a pass in their exams. I managed that, but it was definitely my one and only teaching triumph. I can't imagine why I ever thought I could be a teacher.

So, that's about it, Frankie, just about up to date. Oh, one more thing you were right about. The earthquake effect. It has stayed with me. Sometimes if I hear a rumble of thunder or a table shakes for no apparent reason, I feel my heart beat faster for a moment. I suppose the earth moving on its axis is bound to leave some remnant of panic. But, on the whole, feeling the earth move is a wonderful thing.

I'll say no more.

Love,

Verity

All my books can be found, sampled and bought with a click from my website:-

www.katefitzroy.co.uk

ROMANTIC THRILLERS

Perfume of Provence   Provence Love Legacy

Provence Flame   Provencal Landscape of Love

Provence Starlight   Provence Snow

Dreams of Tuscany   Moonlight in Tuscany

Love on an Italian Lake

WINE DARK MYSTERIES

Well Chilled Case 1   Skin Contact Case 2:

Lingering Finish Case 3

Rich Earthy Tuscany Case 4:

Mistaken Identities Case 5:   Fine Racy Wine Case 6:

Horizontal Tasting Case 7   Full Bodied Lush Case 8:

Pink Fizz Case 9:   Fresh and Fruity Case 10:

Juicy Ruby Case 11:   Lay Down Case 12:

Printed in Great Britain
by Amazon